James Hadley Chase and The Murder Room

>>> This title is part of The Murder Room, our series dedicated to making available out-of-print or hard-to-find titles by classic crime writers.

Crime fiction has always held up a mirror to society. The Victorians were fascinated by sensational murder and the emerging science of detection; now we are obsessed with the forensic detail of violent death. And no other genre has so captivated and enthralled readers.

Vast troves of classic crime writing have for a long time been unavailable to all but the most dedicated frequenters of second-hand bookshops. The advent of digital publishing means that we are now able to bring you the backlists of a huge range of titles by classic and contemporary crime writers, some of which have been out of print for decades.

From the genteel amateur private eyes of the Golden Age and the femmes fatales of pulp fiction, to the morally ambiguous hard-boiled detectives of mid twentieth-century America and their descendants who walk our twenty-first century streets, The Murder Room has it all. >>>

The Murder Room
Where Criminal Minds |

themurderroom.com

T0352401

James Hadley Chase (1906–1985)

Born René Brabazon Raymond in London, the son of a British colonel in the Indian Army, James Hadley Chase was educated at King's School in Rochester, Kent, and left home at the age of 18. He initially worked in book sales until, inspired by the rise of gangster culture during the Depression and by reading James M. Cain's *The Postman Always Rings Twice*, he wrote his first novel, *No Orchids for Miss Blandish*. Despite the American setting of many of his novels, Chase (like Peter Cheyney, another hugely successful British noir writer) never lived there, writing with the aid of maps and a slang dictionary. He had phenomenal success with the novel, which continued unabated throughout his entire career, spanning 45 years and nearly 90 novels. His work was published in dozens of languages and over thirty titles were adapted for film. He served in the RAF during World War II, where he also edited the RAF Journal. In 1956 he moved to France with his wife and son; they later moved to Switzerland, where Chase lived until his death in 1985.

By James Hadley Chase
(published in The Murder Room)

Tell it to the Birds

James Hadley Chase

An Orion book

Copyright © Hervey Raymond 1963

The right of James Hadley Chase to be identified as the author of this
work has been asserted in accordance with the Copyright, Designs and
Patents Act 1988.

This edition published by
The Orion Publishing Group Ltd
Orion House
5 Upper St Martin's Lane
London WC2H 9EA

An Hachette UK company
A CIP catalogue record for this book is available from the British Library

ISBN 978 1 4719 0351 9

www.orionbooks.co.uk

For John Hale

I dedicate this book to you as a token of appreciation for
all you have done for me

J. H. C.

PART ONE

1

At the far end of the narrow road, scarcely wide enough to take two cars and bordered by high prickly hedges, Anson finally found the house he had been looking for for the past hour. The house hid behind a barrier of overgrown shrubs that stood either side of shabby double gates. It wasn't until Anson got out of his car and approached the gates that he had his first glimpse of the house. He didn't immediately look at it because his attention became riveted on the garden. Although quite small with a twenty-foot square lawn as immaculate as the surface of a billiard table, the garden presented a horticultural picture seldom seen outside professional floral exhibitions.

Everything, including a miniature fountain, a tiny waterfall, massed bedding plants, blazing with colour, standard roses in perfect bloom, flowering shrubs and even a dovecot was there.

For several moments, Anson stood at the gate staring at the garden, then he looked beyond the garden to the house.

By comparison, the house was as surprising as the garden. It was a two-storey brick and wooden structure with a red tiled roof. At one time, the wooden face of the house had been painted a dark green, but the rain, the wind and the sun over the years had played havoc with the paintwork, and the house now presented a shabby, neglected and uncared-for appearance. The windows were streaked with dust and dirt. The brass doorknocker was black with grime. To the left of the house was a two-car garage with a broken window and many of its roof tiles missing.

Anson looked at the garden, then at the house, then at the garden again. He stepped back and read the name painted in crude white letters on the gate: "Mon Repose".

He zipped open the well-worn leather document case he was carrying and took from it a letter he had received that morning. He read it again:

Mon Repose.

Nr Pru Town

National Fidelity Insurance Corporation
Brent
Dear Sir,

I would be glad if your representative would call between two and four o'clock any afternoon this week.

I have a few pieces of jewellery worth about $1,000 which my husband thinks I should insure against theft or loss.

    Yours, etc.
    Meg Barlowe.

Anson pushed open the gates, drove the car onto the tarmac drive, then walked up the drive to the house.

Heavy rain clouds hovered threateningly overhead. The sun, obscured by the clouds, made a faint, brave light over the spectacular garden. In an hour or so, Anson thought, as

2

he reached for the dirt-grimed knocker, it would be pouring with rain. He lifted the knocker and rapped twice.

There was a pause, then he heard quick footfalls; the door opened.

Anson remembered to the moment of his death his first meeting with Meg Barlowe.

At the age of fourteen, Anson had his first sexual experience. His parents had gone on a short trip, leaving him in charge of the hired help: a woman some twenty years older than Anson: plain, fat and a Quaker. His parents had been gone less than four hours when the woman had come into Anson's bedroom where he had been lolling on the bed, reading a lurid paperback. Half an hour later, Anson had moved from his youth to corrupt manhood, and from then on, the sexual hunt was ever present in his alert, active mind. This first experience left him with a conviction that didn't last long, that all women were easy. Later, when he discovered his error, he preferred to consort with prostitutes rather than be bothered to persuade and woo. He was fastidious in his choice, and the women he went with cost him a considerable amount of his weekly earnings.

Beside this constant sexual urge, Anson had yet another weakness: a persistent and incurable urge to gamble. He had little luck. The combination of paying for his sexual pleasures and losing to his bookmaker had him continually struggling to keep solvent.

His shrewdness, personality and drive had gained him a Field Agency of the National Fidelity Insurance Corporation that covered three small prosperous towns: Brent, Lambsville and Pru Town. This district offered a rich field for an energetic insurance salesman. It was a farming district, and most farmers owned two or three cars, were interested in life insurance and anxious to insure their crops and property. But what Anson earned, he threw away until he was now facing a financial crisis that alarmed even his irresponsible conscience.

Before leaving Brent for his weekly visit to Pru Town and Lambsville, he had received a telephone call from Joe Duncan, his bookmaker.

In his wheezy asthmatic voice, Duncan had said, "Listen, Anson, you know what you owe me?"

Anson had said, "Sure, Joe. Relax. You'll get paid."

"You owe me close on a thousand bucks," Duncan said. "You settle on Saturday. If you don't, Sailor will be around to talk to you."

Sailor Hogan was Joe Duncan's debt collector. At one time he had been the light heavyweight champion of California. His viciousness was legend. If he failed to collect a debt, he left a permanent mark on the welsher.

But Anson wasn't worried about a mere thousand dollars. If the worst came to the worst, he could scrape that amount up by borrowing from his friends, selling his TV set and even hocking his car, but the pressure was now on, and as he hung up, he remembered he owed Sam Bernstein, the local moneylender, eight thousand dollars and he had to the end of the year to settle or else ... When he had signed the IOU back in June, next June seemed a long way off. He had plunged the whole of the borrowed money on a rank outsider at 100 to 1 from a tip straight from the stable boy and the horse had turned out to be exactly what it was: a rank outsider.

This day was Tuesday. Anson had five more days ahead of him in which to find a thousand dollars to keep Duncan quiet. This wasn't an impossible task, but he flinched from the thought of how to raise eight thousand dollars for Bernstein. But here, at least he had time.

Because he was now getting anxious, Anson was a little too persistent, a little too pressing, and when a salesman gets into that state of mind, he doesn't and never will sell insurance.

This week had begun badly, but he was a salesman enough and optimistic enough to assure himself it should finish well.

As he lifted the knocker on the shabby, paint-peeled door of this shabby house standing in this extraordinary garden, he had a presentiment that his luck was about to change.

Anson looked at Meg Barlowe as she stood in the doorway, regarding him with her large, searching cobalt-blue eyes.

At the sight of this woman who he judged to be a year or so younger than himself, Anson experienced a rush of blood through his body that inevitably happened when he met any woman who awoke his sexual feelings.

She was tall: an inch or so taller than himself, and built with the strength and durability of a wooden wedge. She had broad shoulders, a provocative bust, a small waist, neat hips and long legs. She wore a close-fitting orange sweater and black tight-fitting slacks. Her auburn coloured hair was caught back with a strip of green ribbon. All this he took in at a glance. She wasn't beautiful. Her mouth was a little too large, and her nose too solid for perfect beauty, but she was the most sensational and sensual looking woman Anson had ever seen.

For a long moment they stared at each other, then her red lips parted as she smiled, showing white, even teeth.

"Good afternoon," she said.

Automatically, but with a conscious effort, Anson moved into his sales approach. His expression, schooled by years of experience, was bright, friendly and alert.

"Mrs Barlowe? I am John Anson. National Fidelity Insurance Corporation. I have a letter from you ..."

"Of course ... do come in."

Still aware that his heart was thumping, Anson followed her through a dark little hall into the living-room.

It was a big room, comfortably furnished. There was a bright log fire burning in the oversized fireplace. Before the fireplace stood a vast settee: large enough to seat four people comfortably. There was an oval shaped table in the bay window. On the table was a portable typewriter and a mass of papers, carbons, and a Webster's Dictionary.

As Anson moved into the room, he became aware of dust and dirt everywhere. The room had the same uncared-for appearance as the exterior of the house.

The woman walked over to the fireplace and now stood, her back to the fire, her hands on her hips, looking at him. Disconcerted by the quizzing expression in her eyes, Anson walked over to the window.

"What a garden you have!" he said. "You must be very proud of it!"

"My husband is." She laughed. "He thinks of nothing else."

Anson turned. His eyes moved over her body.

"Is it his profession?"

"Not exactly. He wants it to be. Right now, he's with Framley's Store in Pru Town. He is in charge of their horticultural department." She waved to the settee. "But do sit down, Mr Anson."

He came around the settee and sat down at the far end, disturbed by being so close to her. She knelt on the seat away from him.

"Phil ... my husband ... he wants me to insure my jewellery," she said. "I don't think that it is worth insuring, but he says it is. What would be the yearly premium?"

"For a thousand dollars?"

"Phil says it is worth that ... I doubt it. But, yes, for a thousand dollars."

Anson became suddenly alert.

"Could I see what you want to insure?"

"Of course ... I'll get it."

He watched her leave the room. She moved gracefully and when she had gone, leaving the door open, he drew in a long slow breath. He sat motionless, staring into the fire, watching the flames flickering around the logs and feeling the heat against his face.

She returned in a few moments with a shabby trinket box. The box contained a dozen pieces of old-fashioned jewellery: the kind of junk found in an antique jeweller's shop: junk bought at auctions in the hope that one piece might be worth the price of the lot.

He looked at her, puzzled.

"Is this all of it?"

She nodded.

"But this isn't worth fifty dollars, let alone a thousand. I guess it isn't even worth fifty dollars."

She laughed and came to sit by his side, taking the box out of his hands.

"I told Phil that and he said you never know with old jewellery. Well, I am sorry to have wasted your time, Mr Anson. I hope you're not mad at me."

Anson could smell the perfume she was wearing. He couldn't place it, but he liked it.

"That's all right." But it wasn't all right. He had wasted an hour getting out here when he might have been doing business in Pru Town. "While I'm here, how are you fixed for insurance? I mean the house ... fire ... burglary?"

"That's all taken care of," Meg said. "This was my husband's mother's house. When she died, she left it to him. Of course, it's all insured. I'm sorry ..."

"That's all right," Anson said. His eyes again moved over her body and he again felt desire stab through him.

"But there is one thing you might help me with now you are here," she went on, paused and looked intently at him.

"Why, sure. What is it?"

He was reluctant to leave. Having her by his side, feeling the warmth of the fire on his face, the shadows lengthening, giving the room an intimate atmosphere, relaxed him.

"I'm writing a short story," she said. "It's to do with insurance." She leaned back, her head resting against the settee, the red reflection from the fire lighting her throat. "It's an idea I had. You might tell me if it would work."

He glanced at the typewriter on the table.

"You write short stories?"

"It gives me something to do. I haven't sold any yet, but you never know." She smiled at him. "Phil doesn't make much money. If I could sell a story ... well, I could buy some clothes." Again she smiled, but he had a sudden idea that she wasn't happy and that idea gave him a feeling of intense excitement. She got to her feet. "If you are going to help me, you deserve a drink. I have only whisky. Will you?"

Anson hesitated. It was just after five o'clock, a little early for drinking, but he found he wanted a drink.

"Why not ... thanks."

8

She was gone only a few minutes, coming back with a bottle of whisky, charge water and ice. She made two stiff drinks. Giving him one of the glasses, she carried the other near to the fire and sat on the floor.

By now the room was becoming dark. She made no attempt to turn on the light. He heard the patter of the rain against the windows, but he paid no attention, his eyes watching her every movement.

"This story I'm working on," she said, looking into the fire, "is about a woman who is desperate for big money. She has a boyfriend who is a ticket clerk at a big airline terminal. This woman has a little money put by and she insures her life for two hundred thousand dollars. She and her boyfriend wait for an air crash out at sea. They have to wait six months before it does happen. Immediately the news is flashed to the terminal, the boyfriend puts the woman's name on the passenger list. He also takes care of the ticket receipt and so on. The woman has moved out of the district where she used to live and is keeping out of sight. He telephones her, warning her of the crash. Then later, her sister puts in a claim for the money showing proof supplied by the boyfriend that the woman, her sister, was on the plane." She paused, took a sip of her drink, then looked at him. "Of course the details have to be worked out, but that's the general idea ... do you think she would get away with it?"

During the twelve years he had been an insurance agent, Anson had become familiar with the tricks and dodges dreamed up by people ambitious to swindle insurance companies. Every week, he received a printed bulletin from Head Office setting out in detail the various swindles attempted. This bulletin came from the Claims Department,

9

run by Maddox who was considered to be the best Claims man in the business.

For the past three months, when money had become so desperately short, Anson had thought of ways and means by which he himself might swindle his company. But for all his shrewdness and experience, he realised he could never succeed unless he had someone on whom he could rely to help him. Even then, there was always Maddox who was said to have a supernatural instinct that told him a claim was a phoney the moment it was laid on his desk.

"It's a nice idea," Anson said. "It might even be believable as fiction, but it would never work in real life."

She looked enquiringly at him.

"But why not?"

"The sum involved is too large. Any claim over fifteen thousand dollars is examined very closely. Suppose this woman insured with my company. The policy would go immediately to the Claims department. The head of this department is a man who has been in the racket for twenty years. During this time, he has had something like five to eight thousand phoney claims to deal with. He has so much experience he can smell a bad claim the way you can smell a dead rat. So what does he do when he gets this policy? He asks himself why a woman should be insuring her life for such a big sum. Who will benefit? Her sister? Why? Is there a boyfriend around? He has twenty experienced investigators who work for him. He'll turn two of them onto this woman. In a few days he will know as much about her as she knows about herself. His men will have unearthed the boyfriend at the air terminal. Once they have dug him up, then God help them both if she is supposed to have died in the air crash. No, it wouldn't work in real life. Make no mistake about that ... not with Maddox around."

10

Meg made a face, then shrugged.

"Oh well! I thought I was onto a good gimmick. I'm disappointed." She drank some of the whisky, then reaching forward, she picked up the poker and stirred the fire into a blaze. "Then it is very difficult to swindle an insurance company?" she asked without looking at him.

Again, Anson felt an intense prickle of excitement run through him.

"Yes ... unless ..."

She was staring into the fire, a little flushed by the heat, her eyes reflecting the red of the flames.

"Unless ...?"

"It could be done, but it needs two people to do it. One couldn't do it."

She twisted around to look at him.

"That makes me think that you have thought about it," she said. "If you do get an idea would you share it with me? I'd write the story and we could go fifty-fifty if I sold it."

He finished his drink, set down the glass and reluctantly got to his feet.

"If I think of anything, I'll call you."

She stood up. They faced each other; again Anson's eyes moved over her body.

"If you do think of something, you could come out here, couldn't you? It's not far from Brent, is it? We could talk over the whole thing and I could get the idea down on paper."

He hesitated, then said what was in his mind: "I guess your husband won't want me around after a day's work."

She nodded.

"You're right. Phil isn't sociable and he hasn't much patience with my writing, but on Monday and Thursday nights he is always at Lambsville. He takes night school there and he stays the night with a friend of his."

11

Anson's hands suddenly turned damp.

"Does he? Well ..."

"So if you get an idea, you'll always find me alone here on those two nights. Don't forget, will you?"

She moved to the door and opened it. Picking up his document case, Anson followed her to the front door. As she opened the door, he said, "By the way, does your husband carry any life insurance?"

"No. He doesn't believe in insurance."

They looked at each other and Anson quickly shifted his gaze.

She went on: "I'm afraid there is no hope for you in that direction. Other salesmen have tried to sell him insurance. He just doesn't believe in it."

Anson stepped out into the rain.

"Thanks for the drink, Mrs Barlowe. If I get an idea for you, I'll call you."

"Thanks. I'm sorry about the jewellery." She gave him a quick smile as she closed the door.

Scarcely feeling the rain on his face, Anson walked down the drive towards his car.

From behind the curtains Meg watched the car drive through the gateway and onto the lane. She watched Anson get out of the car and shut the gate then return to the car. She remained motionless until the sound of the car engine had died away, then she turned swiftly, crossed to the telephone and dialled a number.

There was a short delay, then a man's voice came over the line.

"Yeah? Who is this?"

"Meg. The fish bites."

There was a pause, then the man said, "Hook him first before you crow," and the connection was cut.

2

Anson's weekly routine included two days in Pru Town. He stayed the night in the Marlborough hotel. At one time he had wasted much time in chasing the local prostitutes, but now, from experience and impatience, he had fixed a date with Fay Lawley, an easygoing blonde who worked at a cigar store on Main Street. For sixty bucks and a dinner, she was willing to go with him to his hotel where the desk clerk who knew Anson well, looked the other way as he took her up to his room.

When Anson arrived at the hotel after his first meeting with Meg Barlowe he had every intention of following his usual routine, but while he was shaving he began to compare Fay with Meg and it occurred to him with surprising force what a cheap hustler Fay was. Disconnecting the razor, he sat on the edge of his bed and lit a cigarette. He told himself he had never met another woman to touch Meg, and she had actually invited him to visit her when her husband was away for the night! Surely that could only mean one thing!

The thought of having an affair with her made him breathless. Again he considered Fay's flashy cheapness, her high-pitched giggles and her vulgarity. Acting on the spur of the moment, he reached for the telephone, but there was no answer to Fay's number. Irritated, he hung up and went back into the bathroom to complete his shave.

It was while he was slapping aftershave lotion on his face that he heard movements in his bedroom. Frowning, he went to the bathroom door and found Fay looking through his wallet.

At the sight of him, she dropped the wallet hurriedly back on the chest of drawers.

"Hello sweetie," she said. "I thought I'd surprise you."

Anson looked her over, his face expressionless. A week ago, he had thought Fay Lawley an exciting woman. Now, comparing her with Meg, he saw her shortcomings. She was shabby, overdressed, dyed and sordid.

"You did surprise me," he said, coming into the bedroom. "Or did I surprise you?"

Fay giggled and put her hand to her mouth. It was this movement that Anson was so used to that now drew his attention to her tobacco stained, chipped teeth.

"John, darling," she said, sinking down on the bed, "I have a favour to ask you."

He remained motionless, looking at her.

"I'm in trouble," she went on after a long and awkward pause. "I've got to have a hundred bucks by tomorrow or I'll lose my room. I'm behind in the rent."

A hundred bucks! Anson thought bitterly. She thought that was being in trouble! What would the silly mare do if she owed eight thousand bucks!

"What do you expect me to do about it?" he said, staring at her. "There's more than a hundred bucks walking Main Street. Go out there and earn it."

She looked sharply at him, her green-blue eyes hardening. "That's a nice thing to say, Sweetie!" she said. "I didn't expect that from you. I'm your girlfriend ... remember?"

He had a sudden urgent desire to be rid of her. If he had had the courage, he would have shoved her out into the corridor and locked the bedroom door, but he was scared she might make a scene. Looking at her, he was horrified with himself for ever having associated with her. Meg now made all his women shabby and sordid.

He went over to his wallet and took out six ten-dollar bills.

"Fay ... I'm sorry. I'm not well. It's something I've eaten," he said. "Here take this ... it's the best I can do. Let's skip tonight. I want to go to bed."

She stared at the bills in his hand, then she looked at him, her eyes quizzing.

"Can't you run to a hundred?" she asked. "I tell you I'm in trouble."

He dropped the bills into her lap.

"Trouble? That's a joke. I'm in trouble too. Be a good girl ... run along. I'm not well."

She put the bills into her shabby handbag and stood up.

"Okay, Sweetie, see you next week."

You're not ever seeing me again, Anson thought. He said, "I'll call you."

He went with her to the door. She paused and looked intently at him.

"Want to change your mind?" She put her hand on him, but he moved quickly back. "Well, okay, if you're as ill as all that ... See you," and she went out into the corridor.

The rest of the evening Anson spent lying on his bed, his thoughts of Meg Barlowe burning holes in his mind.

The following day when he wasn't actually working, he thought about her. His mind still tormented by her, he left Pru Town for Lambsville where he had a few calls to make. He got through his calls by half past five. He had to pass through Pru Town again to reach the Brent highway, and he had to pass the dirt road that led to the lonely, intriguing Barlowe house.

As he drove along the highway, he tried to decide whether he dare call on Meg so soon. She had said she would be alone this night: that her husband would be staying in Pru Town. But suppose she really meant that stuff about a plot for a short story? He would look a dope arriving at the house with no ideas for her if he had misunderstood the set-up and she hadn't after all been extending an invitation to him to share her bed.

He reached the dirt road and pulled up, drawing off the highway onto the grass verge. He sat for some moments, trying to make up his mind what to do.

I'd better not, he thought to himself. It's too risky. I could spoil my chance. It shouldn't be too hard to think up a plot for her and I'll then have a legitimate excuse for calling on her. She'll be on her own again next Monday. Between now and Monday, I should be able to dream up something: it doesn't matter how corny it is, but I can't barge in there without something to tell her.

Reluctantly he started the car engine and drove on to Brent.

"Have you something on your mind, Mr Anson?" Anna Garvin asked curiously.

Anson started, frowned and looked across the office to where Anna sat behind a typewriter. She had been working for him now for the past two years. She was young, fat, cheerful and capable. Apart from wearing heavy horn-rimmed glasses which Anson disliked on women, she also had a talent for wearing all the wrong clothes which made her look more homely and fatter than necessary.

She had interrupted an idea he had been developing: an idea for a story which had to do with an insurance swindle.

"I've spoken to you twice," Anna went on. "You just sit there as if you were hatching a plot to murder someone."

Anson stiffened.

"Look, Anna, I'm busy. Keep quiet, can't you?"

She grimaced, screwing up her good-natured, fat face, then she went on with her typing.

Anson got to his feet and crossed to the window to stare down at the steady stream of traffic passing along Main Street.

This was Saturday morning. After lunch he had arranged to play a round of golf with a friend of his, but he now found himself in no mood for golf. He had Meg on his mind so badly he couldn't concentrate on his work. A dozen or so letters lay on his desk, waiting his attention, but he couldn't bring himself to bother with them.

... as if you were hatching a plot to murder someone.

And that was exactly what he had been doing: planning a murder for gain, but, of course, only for this story he was working out for Meg Barlowe. Just suppose he had really been planning a murder. Was he so transparent that someone as simple as Anna could read his thoughts?

He forced himself to his desk.

"Let's go," he said and when Anna picked up her notebook, Anson began to dictate.

Anson had a one-room apartment on the fourth floor of the Albany Arms, a block of apartments near the Brent railroad station. He had lived in this rabbit warren of a place since he had become the Field Agent for the Insurance Corporation. Each apartment was provided with a garage which was situated in the basement of the building and approached by a long drive-in from the road.

Anson had played bad golf, had had an indifferent dinner, but he had had a lot to drink. Now, relaxed from the exercise and slightly drunk, he drove his car down the dimly lit drive-in and expertly swung the car into the stall allotted to him. He noticed that most of the other stalls were empty. This was the weekend. There was always a rush to get out of Brent over the weekend, and Anson liked the quiet that prevailed in the apartment block, free from the racket of television, people walking over his head and children screaming and quarrelling in the courtyard.

He cut the engine, turned off the headlights and got out of the car. As he slammed the car door shut, he became aware that he wasn't alone. He looked sharply to his right.

A tall, thick-set man had appeared out of the shadows and was now standing looking at him from the entrance of the stall. His unexpected appearance gave Anson a start. He stared into the gloom, looking towards where the man was standing.

"Hi, palsy," the man said in a thick, husky voice. "I've been waiting quite a long time for you to show up."

Anson's heart skipped a beat and he felt a cold clutch of fear. He recognised this threatening, massive figure: Sailor Hogan! During the past days his mind had been so obsessed with Meg Barlowe he had entirely forgotten Joe Duncan's threat. Now he remembered what Duncan had said: *You pay up on Saturday. If you don't, Sailor will be around to talk to you.*

Anson recalled a story he had heard about Sailor Hogan. How he had visited a client of Joe's who had failed to pay up. Sailor had maimed the man ... Anson had actually seen the man after Sailor had dealt with him so he knew the story to be no exaggeration. Sailor, so they said, had laced his thick fingers together and had hit the man a frightful chopping blow on the back of his neck. The man was now going around in a wheelchair, looking and acting like an idiot. When the police had tried to pin the assault onto Sailor, he proved with the help of five bookmakers that he was playing poker with them in Lambsville at the time the assault had taken place.

And now here was Sailor Hogan walking slowly and deliberately towards Anson who backed away. It wasn't until he felt his heels grinding against the concrete wall that Anson came to a standstill. By now, Sailor was within four feet of him. Sailor paused, his hands thrust into his trouser pockets, his shapeless hat cocked over one eye, a cigarette dangling from his thick, moist lips.

"I've come to collect, palsy," he said. "Let's have it."

Anson drew in a quick uneven breath.

"Tell Joe he'll have it on Monday," he said, trying to keep his voice steady.

"Joe said for me to collect it now or else ..." Sailor said and took big, knuckly fists out of his pockets. "Come on, palsy, I want to get home."

Anson felt the cold concrete wall pressing against his shoulders. He could retreat no further. He thought of the man in the wheelchair.

"I'll have the money on Monday," he said. "Tell Joe ... he'll understand. I'm expecting ..." He broke off as Sailor sidled towards him. Suddenly more frightened than he had ever been before, he said in a high hysterical voice. "No! Keep away from me! No!"

Sailor grinned at him.

"Palsy, you're in trouble. When I'm not working for Joe, I work for Sam Bernstein. You owe him eight grand. Sam

19

doesn't think you'll pay him. Okay, you have time, but Sam is worried about you. Joe's worried about you too. You'd better pay Joe on Monday or I'll have to work you over." His small white teeth gleamed in the overhead light as he smiled viciously. "If you don't raise Sam's dough, I'll fix you till you wish you were dead. Understand?"

"Sure," Anson said, feeling cold sweat running down his ribs.

"Okay. You pay Joe on Monday ... that's fixed, huh?" It's going to be all right, Anson thought wildly. I've gained two days. Monday night I'll be with Meg.

But it wasn't all right for Sailor moved forward with a quick, shifting movement that left Anson helpless to defend himself.

Sailor's hammer-like fist sank into Anson's stomach with paralysing and awful violence and sent him forward in a jack-knife dive.

Anson sprawled face down on the oily concrete floor. He heard Sailor say, "Monday, palsy. If you haven't the dough, then you're in for a real beating and remember Sam ... you don't pay him and you're as good as dead."

Anson lay still, his hands clutching his stomach, his breath moaning through his clenched teeth. He was dimly aware of the cold ground that chilled his pain-racked body as he listened to the quick footfalls of the ex-light heavyweight champion of California as he walked briskly up the drive-in and out into the darkness of the night.

Anson lay in bed. The day was Sunday. The time was eleven fifteen a.m. Around his navel where Hogan had sunk his fist the flesh was yellow, green and black. Somehow he had managed to drag himself to the elevator and reach his apartment. He had taken three sleeping tablets and had got into bed. When he woke, the bright morning sunshine was coming around the edges of the blind. He had limped to the bathroom. His guts felt as if they were on fire. At least, he thought, I am not passing blood, but he was frightened. He thought with horror of the next meeting with Hogan if he failed to raise Duncan's money. His mind moved ahead to next June. He must have been out of his mind to have borrowed eight thousand dollars from Bernstein. He must have been crazy to have put all that money on that goddamn horse! He felt a cold chill as he thought of the reckoning. He was certain now that he would never be able to raise that sum. He put his hand to his tender, aching stomach and he cringed. Hogan would fix him. He knew it. He too would be going around looking like an idiot after Hogan had fixed him.

He lay there in a mood of frightened, black despair during the next four hours. His mind darted like a trapped mouse, searching for a way of escape.

There was one thought that kept moving into his mind and which he immediately rejected, but as the hours passed and no other solution presented itself, he finally began to consider the idea.

Up to this moment he had shied away from any criminal act to make money, but now he realised there was nothing left but to make money dishonestly.

He thought of Meg Barlowe.

She has something on her mind, he told himself. That story about an insurance swindle ... she knew that junk she called jewellery was worthless. So why did she ask me to call? Why did she tell me her husband would be away for the night on Mondays and Thursdays? This could be my way out ... this could be the chance I'm looking for.

He was still thinking about the idea when he drifted off into an exhausted sleep that took him through the night to Monday morning.

Anson walked across the vast parking lot of Framley's store with a slight dragging step. Movement caused him pain. He had to force himself to walk upright.

He pushed open the swing doors into the bustle of the store. He looked around, then asked one of the elevator attendants where he could find the horticultural department.

"Basement. Section D," the girl told him.

There was a big crowd around the horticultural stand and Anson wasn't surprised. He recognised the same genius that had created the garden at the Barlowe house. People moved around gaping and exclaiming at the blooms, the perfect floral arrangements, the little fountains and the beautifully arranged banks of cut flowers. There were four girls, wearing green smocks, busy with their order books. Barlowe stood by a desk, a pencil behind his ear, while he watched the girls book orders.

Barlowe was so unlike the man Anson had imagined him to be that after staring at him for several seconds, he asked one of the girls if it was Mr Barlowe. When the girl said he was, Anson moved back to the edge of the crowd. He again studied the man who was now selling a rose tree to an elderly couple.

How in the world could such a sensational looking woman like Meg have come to marry such a man? Anson asked himself. From his vantage point behind the crowd, Anson studied Barlowe with increasing surprise.

Barlowe was in his early forties. He had a shock of thick black hair. He was thin and undersized. His eyes were deep set in hollows that were dark ringed. He had a thin, ill-tempered mouth and his nose was pointed and long. Examining him, Anson decided that this little shrimp of a man's only grace lay in his long, slender and artistic hands: they were beautiful hands, but there was nothing else about him that could win anyone's favour.

Anson moved away from the scent of the flowers, suddenly very confident that he had no serious competition to fear. He even forgot the nagging soreness of his stomach as he passed the parking lot towards his car. He had three prospects to call on. The time was now twenty minutes to four. He should be free to visit Meg by seven o'clock.

On his way to his car, he paused by a row of telephone booths. It took him only a few minutes to find Barlowe's telephone number. He dialled the number.

Meg answered the call. The sound of her voice made him feel breathless.

"Good afternoon, Mrs Barlowe," he said, forcing his voice to sound brisk. "This is John Anson."

There was a pause, then she said, "Who?" He felt a moment of irritation. Didn't she even remember his name?

"John Anson: National Fidelity Insurance. You remember me?"

She said at once, "Why, of course. I'm sorry. I was trying to write ... my mind was miles away."

"I hope I haven't disturbed you."

"Oh, no. I was thinking of you. I was wondering if you had an idea for me."

He was tempted to tell her that he had spent the whole of yesterday thinking of her.

"That's why I am telephoning ... I do have an idea. I was wondering ..." He let it hang, feeling his hand turn moist as he gripped the telephone receiver.

"Yes?" There was a pause as he still said nothing, then she went on, "I suppose you're not free this evening?"

Anson drew in a deep breath.

"I'm in Pru Town right now. I have a few calls to make, but I could drop by around seven o'clock if that would be convenient?"

"Well, why not?" Her voice went up a note. "Come to supper. There won't be much but I hate eating alone."

Anson was suddenly worried that she might hear the violent beating of his heart.

"Fine ... then, around seven," and with an unsteady hand, he put the receiver back onto its cradle.

She was sophisticated, sun-tanned and very sure of herself. She wore a sky-blue shirt and close-fitting white slacks. She paused before Barlowe and stared at him the way you stare at a sudden coffee stain on your best tablecloth.

"Mary Wheatcroft," she said. "Is it too early to plant?" Barlowe felt a tightening in his chest at the sight of this woman.

"Yes ... a little early, but I can take an order. We will deliver and plant when ..."

Her sapphire-blue eyes flicked over him indifferently. "I want two dozen. It's Mrs Van Hertz. I have an account with you ... arrange it for me," and she moved away, her hips rolling under the white material of her slacks.

Barlowe watched her go.

One of the assistants said sharply, "Mr Barlowe ... you have cut yourself!"

Barlowe looked at the blood dripping from his fingers. His grip had unconsciously tightened on the pruning knife he was holding.

His pale brown eyes shifted once again to Mrs Van Hertz's arrogant back. He lifted his hand and licked the warm blood from his fingers.

3

As Anson reached the top of the dirt road, he saw the double gates leading to the Barlowe house were open and so too were the doors of the garage. Taking the hint, he drove his car into the garage, got out, shut the garage doors and then walked back and shut the double gates.

A light was on in the sitting-room. As he walked to the front door, he saw Meg's shadow pass the blind as she crossed the room, to let him in.

She opened the door and for a moment they stood looking at each other.

"You're very punctual," she said. "Come on in."

He followed her into the sitting-room.

In the shaded lamplight, as he took off his overcoat, they again looked at each other. She was wearing a flame coloured dress with a wide, pleated skirt. She was even more sensational looking than when he had first met her.

"Let's eat, shall we?" she said. "Then we can talk. I don't know about you but I'm starving. I've been working all day and haven't bothered to eat since breakfast."

"Sure, I'd like to," he said, aware that he had no appetite. "How's the work going?"

"Oh, so ... so." She waved towards the table. She had pushed aside her typewriter and her papers and had set two plates on which lay some cold cuts of beef and pickles. The cutlery was dumped anyhow. There was a bottle of whisky, ice and charge water at hand. "It's a bit of a picnic. I'm no cook."

They sat down at the table and she poured two stiff drinks.

"So you have an idea for me?" she said, beginning to eat quickly and ravenously. "I'm terribly excited; I do want a good idea."

Anson sipped his drink, then making an effort, he too began to eat.

"It's something we can talk about," he said, paused, then went on, "Mrs Barlowe ... it interests me ... have you been married long?"

She glanced up.

"A year ... the end of the month will be our first anniversary. Why do you ask?"

"I guess I get interested in people's backgrounds. I was in Framley's store this afternoon. Your husband seemed to be very busy."

"He's always busy. He's the original busy bee."

Was there a note of contempt in her voice? Anson wondered, suddenly alert.

"Meeting so many people as I do, I'm often surprised at the odd, unexpected married couples I run into. Seeing your husband, I should never have imagined you would have married him." He paused and looked at her, wondering if he had gone too far. Her reply sent a hot rush of blood up his spine.

"Goodness knows why I did marry the poor fish," she said. "I guess I should have my head examined."

She continued to eat, not looking at him and he stared at her. Then aware of his concentrated stare, she looked up.

"You're not eating ... is there anything wrong?"

He put down his knife and fork.

26

"I haven't been too well over the weekend. I'm sorry. It's just I'm off my food."

"But not your drinking, I hope?"

"No."

"Why not go over to the fire? You don't have to watch me eat. Go on ... I won't be long."

He carried his drink to the settee. He sat down and stared into the flickering flames.

Goodness knows why I did marry the poor fish.

This could be the green light he was hoping for.

"Have I shocked you?" she asked suddenly. "You asked me, so I told you. Phil is a poor fish. All he thinks about is his garden. He has only one ambition: to set himself up as a florist with a greenhouse and to sell flowers. He will never do that because he will never make enough money to find the necessary capital. He would need at least three thousand dollars to start a business of his own."

"I should have thought he would have needed more than that," Anson said.

Meg grimaced.

"You don't know my darling Phil. He thinks small. All he wants is a greenhouse and an acre of land."

"Just why did you marry him?" Anson asked, staring into the fire.

There was a long pause. He could hear her cutting the meat on her plate.

"Why? Ask me another! I thought he had money. I thought I was escaping from the things girls like me want to escape from. Okay ... I made a mistake. Now I'd like to be a widow."

Anson leaned forward. He felt the need of the flickering flames. His body had suddenly turned cold.

27

He heard her push back her chair, then she came and sat near him.

"You're interested in me, aren't you?" she said. "Why?"

"Why?" Anson gripped his glass so tightly his knuckles turned white. "Because I think you are the most exciting woman I have ever met."

She laughed.

"I haven't had anything said to me like that since I was stupid enough to get married."

"Well, there it is. I'm saying it."

"Come to that if we are going to hand out compliments, I think you're pretty nice yourself."

Anson drew in a long, slow breath.

"The moment I set eyes on you I thought you were wonderful," he said. "I've had you on my mind every hour since we first met."

"These things happen, don't they?" She reached for a cigarette, lit it and blew the smoke towards the fire.

"Two people meet: there is a sudden chemical explosion and bingo ...!" She turned her head slowly and looked directly at him, her cobalt-blue eyes inviting. "Don't let's waste time, John. Time is always running out on me. You want to love me, don't you?"

Anson set down his glass.

"Yes," he said huskily.

She flicked her cigarette into the fire.

"Then love me," she said.

A log dropped onto the red-hot bed of ashes and flared up, lighting the room for a brief moment. Meg moved away from Anson and getting down on her knees, she put more logs on the fire and stirred the fire into a blaze.

28

"Like a drink?" she asked, looking over her shoulder at him.

"No ... come back here," Anson said.

She didn't move. Poker in hand, she continued to stir the fire, making lively shadows on the ceiling.

"Look at the time," she said. "It's after nine. Can you stay the night?"

"Yes."

She lit a cigarette, then squatting before the fire, the light from the flickering logs on her face, she went on, "Tell me about this idea of yours ... this idea for a story."

Anson stared up at the moving shadows on the ceiling. He was relaxed and happy. Their lovemaking had been violent, exciting and satisfying. The ghosts of every girl he had made love with slid through his mind: that's all they were now: faded, dull ghosts.

"John ... tell me about your idea," Meg said.

"Yes, all right, I will have a drink."

She made two drinks, gave him a glass and then sat on the floor again before the fire.

"Tell me ..."

"I don't know anything about storytelling, but I think this more or less is how it goes," Anson said, staring at the ceiling. "An insurance salesman needs money badly. One day he calls on a woman who has made an inquiry about a fire coverage. He falls in love with her and she with him. She is unhappily married. He persuades the husband to take out a life policy. Between the two – the salesman and the wife – they concoct a plan to get rid of the husband. Because the salesman knows how to handle the set-up, they get away with it. It is in the working out of the details that the story is interesting." He took a long drink and set down his glass. "Like the idea?"

29

She reached for the poker and again stirred the fire into a blaze.

"It's not very original, is it?" she said doubtfully. "When we first met you said it was very difficult to swindle an insurance company and yet you say these two get away with it."

"It's not only difficult, but dangerous, but the insurance salesman knows how to handle it. If he wasn't in the racket himself, it would be more than dangerous."

"And isn't it contrived?" She put down the poker and turned to look at him. "I mean the reader would have to accept the fact that the husband would be willing to take out an insurance policy. But why should he? What I mean is, suppose it was Phil that was the husband. I know for certain he would never insure his life. He is against taking out an insurance policy."

"That depends of course on how the story is set up," Anson said. "But okay, just for the sake of discussing this, suppose the man was your husband, you were the unhappily married woman and I was the salesman."

There was a short silence, then without looking at him, Meg said, "Well ... all right ... let's just suppose ..."

"I am certain I could sell your husband an insurance policy," Anson said. "It's the way I'd approach him that would hook him ... I'm sure I could do it."

"How would you approach him?"

"Knowing he needs capital," Anson said, "I wouldn't try to sell him a policy as a life insurance. I'd sell him the policy as security to get a loan from the bank. Banks accept life policies as securities for a loan, and as he is so keen to set up on his own, I would have him half sold already."

Meg shifted to a more comfortable position.

"You're clever," she said. "I hadn't thought of that."

"That's only the start of it," Anson said. "I know I wouldn't be able to sell him anything larger than a five thousand dollar coverage. That's not much good, is it? It's all right for him: he could raise a three thousand dollar loan on that coverage, but if he died suddenly, it wouldn't be much use to you, would it?"

She shook her head, staring into the fire.

"It wouldn't be much use to me either, but fifty thousand dollars would be ... wouldn't it?"

She looked at him.

"Yes, but ..."

"The trick in this is I could insure him for fifty thousand and he would imagine he was insured only for five thousand."

Again there was a long pause, then Meg said, "It's beginning to be interesting. Just suppose Phil did take out an insurance coverage for fifty thousand dollars ... then what happens?"

Here was the danger spot of the plan, Anson thought. He would now have to move very carefully. Maybe he was rushing this too fast.

"Don't let's keep this story on such a personal basis," he said. "I was using your husband because it makes it more believable. Let's now imagine, shall we, we have a man – any man – insured for fifty thousand dollars although he doesn't know it ... his wife and an insurance salesman who are in love with each other ... okay?"

"Yes ... of course."

"These two are in love and they need money. If the husband dies, the wife will get fifty thousand dollars, which she will share with her lover, but it isn't going to be that easy because the husband shows no signs of dying. So these two begin to think about how to get rid of him. The wife

31

mustn't have anything to do with the ... the getting rid of the husband. That would be completely fatal. His death must appear to be an accident without the wife being involved in any way."

"You've really thought about this, haven't you, John?" she said, looking at him, her cobalt eyes intent. "Go on ... so what happens?"

"Suppose the husband is keen on gardening. Suppose he has a miniature pond," Anson said, his voice a little husky. "One Saturday afternoon, the wife goes down to the shops, leaving her husband working in the garden. He falls off a ladder and hits his head on the side of the pond ... his face goes into the water and when the wife returns, she finds him drowned. Of course, what really happened is the insurance salesman has knocked the husband over the head and drowned him in the pond."

Neither of them looked at each other. Anson felt rather than saw Meg suppress a shudder. She said, "But what about this man you were talking about ... Maddox? The man in charge of the Claims department?"

Anson took another drink. He had nothing to worry about now, he told himself. She was ready to co-operate with him. She had abruptly brought the story back into real life by mentioning Maddox. She was ready to be rid of her husband. He was sure of that if he could convince her he could do it with safety and with profit.

"Yes: there's Maddox. We mustn't underestimate him. He's dangerous, but he does think in a groove. Man and wife: man insures his life for fifty thousand dollars and suddenly dies. How about the wife? That's the way his mind works. It is essential to our plan that you have a cast-iron alibi. He must be absolutely convinced that you couldn't have had anything to do with your husband's death. Once he is convinced of that, he'll let the claim go through. I can convince him."

She picked up the poker and stirred the fire.

"So if I went into Pru Town while you ... you handled Phil, it would be all right?" she asked, as calmly and as casually as if they were discussing a movie they had seen.

"That's the way I see it," Anson said. He finished the whisky and sat up. "Do you like the idea?"

She turned slowly and stared at him.

"Oh, yes, John, I like it. If only you knew how this drab life with him is crushing me! Fifty thousand dollars! I can't believe it ... all that money and my freedom!"

Anson felt a chill of uneasiness run through him. This was too easy, he thought. She has either been planning to murder Barlowe for months or she doesn't realise what she is getting into. It's too easy.

"The money would come to you," he said, looking intently at her. "I would have to trust you to share it with me. I need the money badly, Meg."

She got to her feet.

"Let's go upstairs."

The expression in her eyes wiped out his uneasiness.

Somewhere downstairs a clock chimed five. Through the open window, the first grey light of the dawn made light enough for Anson to look around the shabby bedroom.

He grimaced at its poverty, and then looked at Meg, lying by his side. The grey light softened her features. She looked younger and even more beautiful.

"Meg ..."

She stirred, murmured something and her hand touched his naked chest.

"Asleep?"

She opened her eyes and looked blankly at him, then she smiled.

"Not really ... dozing ..."

"Me too." He slid his arm around her, pulling her to him. "I've been thinking; you really want to go ahead with this thing? It's not just something you're imagining is going to happen in one of your stories?"

"I want to go ahead with it. I can't go on living this way. I must have money ..."

"That's the way I feel, but it won't be easy. There is a lot to think about. We've only just started; we're only on the fringe of this thing."

She was now fully awake and she sat up.

"I'll get some coffee. Let's talk. We may not get the chance again ... not to have a real talk."

She was right of course. After this, he knew he would have to be very careful about seeing her again. If Maddox ever found out they were lovers, the plan forming in his mind would be cooked.

He waited for her, listening to her moving around downstairs. She came back eventually with coffee and set the tray on a table by the bed.

She had on a pale green nylon nightdress that was completely transparent, but now Anson could look at her without feeling the desperate urge to possess her, for their lovemaking had been long and satisfying.

She poured a cup of coffee and gave it to him.

"If we do it ... you're sure it will work?" she asked, sitting on the edge of the bed while she poured herself a cup.

Her attitude not only made him uneasy, but it irritated him. She couldn't be so utterly cold-blooded as she

34

sounded, he thought. She just didn't realise what they were planning.

"No, I'm not sure," he said, determined to make her realise the danger of this thing. "It will take time. I'll have to plan every move. But first I want to be absolutely certain you're really willing ... you really want to do this thing."

She made an impatient movement.

"Of course I do."

"Do you realise what we are planning to do?" Anson paused, then went on, speaking slowly and deliberately, "We are going to commit a murder! Do you realise that?"

He was watching her. Her expression hardened, but she didn't flinch.

"You heard me, Meg? We are going to commit murder!"

"I know." She looked at him, her mouth set in a determined line. "Does it frighten you?"

He drew in a deep breath.

"Yes ... it frightens me. Doesn't it frighten you?"

Again she made an impatient movement.

"I can't even feel sorry for him. I've had to live with him for nearly a year. I've thought for months now how happy I could be if he were dead ..."

"You could have divorced him," Anson said, staring at her.

"Where would that get me? At least I have a roof and food – no other woman but a mug like me would look at him ... and now I won't have him near me. You don't imagine he sleeps in this bed, do you? I lock him out. I've locked him out ever since our first horrible night together. You don't know ... he's vile ... he's ..." She stopped and grimaced. "I'm not talking about it. Some men have these kinks ... he has ... I'll be glad when he's dead!"

35

Anson relaxed. Now he could understand her indifference. At last, he had found someone he could work with. This woman wouldn't let him down.

"I'm sorry," he said. "I didn't know it was as bad as that. Well, all right ... we'll use him, but you must think about it. If I make a mistake, you'll be involved. Don't kid yourself the jury will be kind to you. A woman who helps to murder her husband for gain gets a pretty rugged time."

"Why should you make a mistake?"

Anson smiled mirthlessly.

"Murder is a funny thing. You can plan carefully and you can be awfully smart, but you can still make a mistake and you have only to make one mistake."

"Is that what you are going to do?" She put down her cup and lit a cigarette. "I don't think so, John. I have faith in you. I think you're clever enough not to make a mistake."

"Have you any money?" he asked abruptly. "I want three thousand dollars if I'm going to work this the way it has to be worked."

"Three thousand dollars?" She stared at him. "I haven't even twenty dollars to call my own."

He had expected that. He had thought it would be too good to be true if she had the money he needed.

"All right ... forget it ... I'll get it somehow."

"But why do you want three thousand dollars?" she asked curiously, staring at him.

Anson felt an impulse to be dramatic. He flicked aside the sheet so she could see the horrible bruise that discoloured the skin of his stomach.

Meg caught her breath.

"What happened? That must be terribly painful, John! What happened?"

36

He flicked the sheet over himself. Her concern made the encounter with Hogan now trifling.

Staring up at the ceiling he told her about Hogan and he told her about Bernstein.

"I'm in trouble," he concluded. "I must have money. For months now I have been hunting for a way out. Now I have found you. The two of us will escape together at the cost of a man's life."

"You owe this bookmaker a thousand ... why do you need three thousand?" Meg asked.

"I need two thousand to cover the first premium on a fifty thousand dollar life policy," Anson told her. "Until the first premium is paid, we can't even think about how we can get rid of your husband. So ... somehow ... I have to raise three thousand dollars." He leaned back against the pillows, looking out of the dirt-grimed window at the rising sun. "I'll have to steal it." He looked at her and grinned. "One thing leads to another, doesn't it? When you get involved in murder, you go the whole way or you don't go at all."

"Steal it? What do you mean?"

He put his hand on her thigh.

"Just that. I must have three thousand dollars. It shouldn't be difficult. I'm committed now. I must find some way to get it." There was a pause, then as she said nothing, but stared quizzingly at him, he went on, "What kind of man is your husband business-wise?"

She made a contemptuous movement.

"All he thinks about ... apart from sex ... is flowers."

"Suppose he has papers to sign? Would he read all the details, including the small print? Is he cautious about what he signs? Some people read every word: others sign without reading anything. This is important. Would he want to read every word of an insurance policy before he signed?"

"No, but he would never sign an insurance policy."

"Just suppose he had a policy in front of him with three or maybe four copies ... would he check them all?"

"He wouldn't. He's not like that."

Anson finished his coffee and set down the cup.

"That's all I want to know ... it'll do for a start." He leaned forward and pulled her down beside him. "You really want to go ahead with this thing, Meg? Once you're in it, there'll be no turning back."

She ran her fingers through his blond hair.

"Why do you keep doubting me?" she asked. "I said I'll do it with you. Don't you understand? To have you and all that money, I'll take any risk."

In the silence of the bedroom with the first rays of the sun striking the dusty mirror above the dressing-table, feeling her fingers caressing through his hair and down the back of his neck, Anson was stupid enough to believe her.

It was while he was eating an underdone egg and burned toast that Anson happened to notice something in a frame, hanging on the wall opposite to where he was sitting.

"What's that?" he asked, pointing a buttery knife. "What's that on the wall?"

Meg was sipping coffee. The time was ten minutes past eight. She was now wearing a shabby green wrap that was none too clean. Her hair was tousled, but in spite of the lack of make-up, she still looked sensually and excitingly beautiful.

She glanced in the direction to which he was pointing.

"Oh, that's Phil's. He's very proud of it. It's a certificate for shooting. Phil is quite a shot."

38

Anson pushed back his chair and crossed the room and examined the ornate certificate in its black frame. He read that the certificate had been awarded by the Pru's Town Small Arms and Target Club to Philip Barlowe for winning the first prize in the .38 revolver shooting tournament held last March.

Anson walked thoughtfully back to the table. He sat down and pushed aside his half-eaten egg. His expression was so thoughtful that Meg looked enquiringly at him.

"What is it, John?"

"So he shoots," Anson said.

"Not now, but he used to. He hasn't done any shooting for nearly a year. I wish he would go to his dreary club. He would be out of my way."

"He owns a gun?" Anson asked.

"Yes," Meg said, frowning. "What's on your mind now, John?"

"Is the gun here ... in the house?"

"Yes." She nodded to the ugly sideboard. "In there."

"I would like to see it."

"See it? But why?"

"May I see it?"

She shrugged, got to her feet and went to the sideboard. She pulled open a drawer and took from it a wooden box which she put on the table.

Anson opened the box to find it contained a .38 police Special, a spare clip and a box of cartridges.

He lifted the gun from the box, checked to see it was unloaded, then balanced it in his hand.

"He doesn't use it now?" he asked.

"He hasn't touched it for months. Why the interest?"

"Do you think it would be safe if I borrowed it for a night?"

She stiffened.

"But why?"

"Could I borrow it?"

"Yes ... of course, but you must tell me ... why?"

"Use your head," Anson said impatiently. He put the gun in his hip pocket. "I have to find three thousand dollars."

She sat motionless, staring at him.

He took six cartridges from the box and dropped them into his pocket.

There was a long pause, then he reached out and pulled her to him. His hands moved down her long back as he pressed his lips to hers.

4

Sometime during the late afternoon, Anson drove into the Caltex Service Station on the Brent highway. While the attendant was filling his tank and cleaning his windshield, Anson went into the office and through to the toilet. He left the toilet door ajar and standing against the far wall, he examined the office. There was a desk, a filing cabinet and a big, old-fashioned safe. He noticed the two big windows that faced the highway.

He moved out of the toilet, satisfied he now had the geography of the office set in his mind and he returned to the car.

As he paid the attendant, he said casually, "You keep open all night, don't you?"

"That's a fact, but I go off in three hours. My sidekick does the night shift."

A few months back, Anson had talked with the manager of the Service station about insuring the takings. He knew there was anything from three thousand to four thousand dollars in the safe. While he had been examining Barlowe's gun, it had flashed through his mind that the Service station could be a pretty easy hold-up.

He was surprised that he felt so calm about planning this robbery. The weight of the gun in his hip pocket gave him a lot of confidence. He decided around four o'clock in the morning, he would walk into the Service station and force the attendant at gunpoint to open the safe. With any luck he would then have enough money to pay off Joe Duncan and to pay the first premium of Barlowe's fifty thousand dollar life policy.

Back at the Marlborough hotel, Anson went up to his room. Sitting on his bed, he examined Barlowe's gun. He knew something about guns as he had served his two years of military service. He satisfied himself that the gun was in good working order, then he loaded it with the six cartridges he had in his pocket. He put the gun in his suitcase.

He then went down to the bar. After drinking two stiff whiskies, he went along to the restaurant. He ordered dinner and asked for half a bottle of claret. He seldom drank wine, but he wanted the cork from the bottle: the cork was to play a minor part in his robbery plan. His stomach still felt sore and he had no appetite. He merely picked at his food. Around nine o'clock, he signed the bill. He put the cork from the wine bottle into his pocket and leaving the restaurant, he walked to the men's toilet room. There was an old negro attendant, dozing in a chair. He peered sleepily at Anson and seeing he needed no service, he closed his eyes again.

Anson washed his hands, and while he did so, he looked in the mirror at the rows of hats and coats hanging on the rack behind him. He picked on a well-worn brown and green striped overcoat; a shabby but distinctive coat, and a Swiss hat with a gay feather in it on the next peg.

After drying his hands, he looked at the dozing negro who had begun to snore gently. Anson took the hat and coat and left the hotel by a side entrance.

Carrying the hat and coat, he walked the few yards down the street to where he had parked his car. He opened the trunk tossed in the hat and coat, closed the trunk and returned to the hotel.

Back in his room, he stretched out on his bed, lit a cigarette and went over in his mind the plan to make sure he knew exactly what he was going to do.

It seemed simple and straightforward so long as he didn't lose his nerve. He would leave the hotel by the staff entrance around three o'clock a.m. At that time he wasn't likely to run into anyone. There was a lay-by near the Service station. He would leave his car there.

He would then darken his blond eyebrows and the sides of his hair with burnt cork, put on the Swiss hat and the borrowed topcoat, tie a handkerchief over the lower part of his face and walk to the Service station. Once he had the money, he would put the telephone out of action and return to his car. If anyone tried to act like a hero ... well, he had the gun.

He got off the bed feeling restless and excited. It was only ten o'clock. He wondered what Meg was doing. She hadn't been far from his thoughts during the day. He went down to the bar, and seeing two salesmen he knew, he joined them.

It was around one o'clock when he returned to his room. He was a little drunk and in a reckless mood. He took Barlowe's gun from the suitcase and sitting on the bed, he balanced the gun in his hand.

This is it, he thought. There is a time when every man worth a nickel must make up his mind what to do with his life. I've put off my decision long enough. I'll never get anywhere without money. With Meg to help me and with fifty thousand dollars to get me started, I'll reach up and take the sun out of the sky.

But he knew he was kidding himself. He knew in a year, probably less, the fifty thousand dollars would be gone. He had never been able to hold onto money. He knew Meg was an exciting sexual plaything, but nothing more, and she would never help him. She was a slut: shiftless and worthless, and like him, money loving.

Well, all right, he said shrugging, the money may not last long, but we'll have a fine time while it does last. He lay back on the pillow, nursing the gun and thinking again of Meg.

Harry Weber had been working the night shift at the Caltex Service station for the past two years. It was a soft job, and Harry liked it. He was an avid reader and the job gave him the opportunity to indulge himself.

After one o'clock a.m. he considered himself busy if he had to service more than three cars up to the time he came off duty which was at seven o'clock a.m. He sometimes wondered why the Service station kept open all night, but as he could relax and read, it was no skin off his nose if they were willing to pay him good money just to sit on his backside and soak himself in the paperbacks on which he spent most of his wages.

A few minutes to four, Harry made himself a jug of coffee. Cup in hand, he settled back in his chair to continue a James Bond story when the glass door to the office swung silently open.

Harry looked up, stiffened, then very slowly set down his cup of coffee on the desk. The paperback slipped out of his hand and dropped to the floor.

The man facing him was wearing an odd looking topcoat and a Swiss style hat. The lower part of his face was hidden by a white handkerchief. In his right hand he held a vicious looking gun that he pointed to Harry.

For a brief moment the two men stared at each other then the gunman said quietly, "Don't act like a hero! I don't want to kill you, but I will if I have to. Get that safe open and pronto!"

"Sure," Harry said, badly shaken. He got slowly and unsteadily to his feet.

The gunman came into the office and crossed to the toilet, his gun still covering Harry. He pushed open the door and backed into the dark little room.

"Get the safe open!" he said, standing in the doorway. "Hurry it up!"

Harry pulled open the top drawer of the desk. Lying by the safe key was a .45 automatic supplied by the Service station for just such an emergency as this. He looked down at the gun and hesitated. Could he grab the gun and shoot before this gunman shot him?

Watching him, Anson saw his hesitation and warning instinct told him there was a gun in the drawer.

"Don't move!" he yelled. "Get back ... get your hands up!"

The note in his voice frightened Harry. Cursing himself for hesitating and yet glad of it, he lifted his hands and backed away.

Anson moved forward, reached into the drawer, took out the gun and then stepped back into the toilet. He put the gun on the floor at his feet.

"Get the safe open!" he said, a snarl in his voice. "Start acting like a hero and I'll kill you!"

Harry took the key and opened the safe.

Anson glanced anxiously through the wide windows and out on to the dark highway.

"Get over against the wall!" he ordered. "Face the wall and don't move."

Harry obeyed.

Anson knelt before the safe and pulled out a large steel cash box. It was unlocked. He opened it. The pile of bills in the box made his eyes gleam. As he began stuffing the bills into his topcoat pockets, he heard the unexpected sound of an approaching motorcycle engine.

His heart skipped a beat. This could only be a traffic cop coming. Would he stop or would he pass the Service station?

Working frantically, Anson stuffed the rest of the bills into his pockets, threw the cash box back into the safe and slammed the safe door shut. He stepped back into the toilet.

"Sit at the desk," he said to Harry, his voice tense and vicious. "Quick! Give me away and you'll get it first!"

Harry was moving towards the desk as the beam of the motorcycle headlight flashed across the office. A moment later the sound of the motorcycle engine spluttered to silence.

A trickle of cold sweat ran down Anson's face. The cop had stopped. He would be coming in!

"If there's any shooting," Anson said, "remember, you'll get it first," and he pushed the door of the toilet so it stood ajar. He could only see part of the office now and it worried him he couldn't see Harry.

As the toilet door pushed to, Harry picked up a pencil and quickly wrote on a bill pad: *Hold up. Gunman in toilet.*

The office door swung open, and a big red-faced cop walked in. He often passed at this time and Harry always had a cup of coffee ready for him.

"Hi, Harry," the cop said cheerfully. "Got any java for your old pal?"

Anson looked around the dark little toilet for a way of escape but he saw immediately he was trapped. The window was too high and too small for him to use.

He heard Harry say, "I've just made some, Tom." The cop pulled off his gauntlet gloves and as he dropped them on the desk, Harry who was now standing, pointed to the written message.

The cop wasn't bright. He frowned down at the message, saying "What's this? Something you want me to read?"

Hearing this, Anson knew he had been betrayed. Again he was surprised how calm he felt. Silently, he opened the door of the toilet room.

Harry saw him and went white. The cop, frowning, was staring at the written message, then he looked round and saw the masked gunman.

"Hold it!" Anson exclaimed, his voice unnaturally high. He lifted the gun so it pointed directly at the cop.

The cop's small eyes widened with shock, then he recovered and slowly he straightened. He looked enormous and threatening to Anson.

"Get back against the wall," Anson said. "Go on ... the pair of you!"

Harry hurriedly moved back until his shoulders were flat against the wall, but the cop didn't move.

"You can't get away with this, punk," he said in a hard, gritty voice. "Give me the rod. Come on ... you can't get away with it."

Anson had a sudden feeling of sensual excitement. This stupid hunk of meat was going to be brave. He watched as the cop held out an enormous hand. He heard him say again, "Hand it over ... come on!" As if he were talking to a circus dog.

47

Anson didn't move. His finger steadily took up the slack of the trigger. Then as the cop began a brave and slow advance, Anson became aware that there was no more slack to take up. The bang of the exploding gun and the kick of it in his hand startled him. He stepped back, drawing in a quick gasping breath. He watched the red of the cop's face suddenly drain from under the coarse weather-beaten skin and the massive legs buckle as if the bones had turned into jelly.

Anson stood motionless, the handkerchief covering the lower part of his face was wet with sweat. He watched the bulky body slide to the floor. One massive hand feebly caught the edge of the desk, spilled off it and then the cop was lying face down at Anson's feet.

Anson started towards the door, paused, grabbed the telephone and wrenched it from the wall. He threw it viciously at Harry who had his hands covering his head, his nerve broken by the shooting.

Anson ran out into the night. With the weight of the money in his pockets flapping against his legs, he fled towards his car.

The following morning, immediately after he had had breakfast, Anson went into the writing room of the hotel and wrote a cheque for $1,045 in favour of Joe Duncan. He put this cheque into an envelope with a curt note saying he would no longer bet with Duncan, sealed the envelope, and then, leaving the writing room, he went to one of the telephone call boxes and telephoned Meg.

There was some delay before she answered and when she did, she sounded cross. The time was twenty minutes to nine and Anson guessed he had got her out of bed.

"I'm coming out this afternoon," he said. "I have something I borrowed to return. Will you be in?"

"Oh, it's you." She still sounded cross. "You woke me up!"

With the vision of the cop falling like a felled tree still in his mind, Anson said impatiently, "Will you be in?"

"Yes ... of course."

"Then around three," and he hung up.

He left the hotel and went over to the Pru Town National bank. He paid in one thousand dollars in cash. The money, he told the teller, was to be credited immediately to his account at Brent. He then registered the letter to Duncan and posted it.

He had five calls to make. He sold a policy worth a thousand dollars to a farmer. Until lunchtime he tried to convince two other prospects why they should insure with the National Fidelity but without success. He then returned to Pru Town for lunch. He bought the lunch edition of the *Pru Town Gazette* and read about the robbery and the shooting at the Caltex Service Station. He learned the cop's name was Tom Sanquist. He had been shot through the lungs and his condition was so critical his wife and twelve-year-old son were at his bedside.

There was a picture of Harry Weber pointing to the toilet where the gunman had hidden. Lieutenant H Jenson, Homicide department at Brent, had been called to the scene.

Anson put down the newspaper and ordered lunch. He was pleased to find that he was hungry. The soreness of his stomach had faded and he was able to enjoy the rather heavy lunch the restaurant provided.

The waiter who served him was full of the robbery and Anson listened politely to what he had to say.

49

"They should never keep such sums in a place as isolated as that," the waiter said as he gave Anson his bill. "It is asking for trouble."

Anson agreed and left the restaurant. In the lobby, he ran into the two salesmen he had been drinking with the previous night. They too had to discuss the robbery.

"Some thug passing through," one of them said. "It's my bet he wasn't a local man. He's miles away by now."

Anson agreed and went on to where he had parked his car. He made another call to renew a car insurance policy. As time was moving on, he drove out to the Barlowe house.

As he drove along the highway, he went over in his mind the events of the previous night. He could see no reason why the police could possibly get on to him. Weber's description of the robber had been influenced by his shaken nerves. He said the man was heavily built and tall which Anson was not. He had described the Swiss hat accurately but he had said the topcoat had been fawn coloured. Sanquist the dying cop, was too ill to be questioned.

On his way back to Pru Town after the robbery, Anson had stopped the car by a wooded thicket and had dumped the hat and topcoat. The robbery had netted him $3,670, more than he had hoped for.

He was still surprised that he was so calm about the whole affair: even the shooting of Sanquist left him unmoved.

As he drove onto the tarmac drive of the Barlowe house, Meg came to the door.

He came towards her, smiling.

"Hello," he said. "Here I am again."

She gave ground, standing aside. Although she returned his smile, her smile didn't reach her eyes. She looked pale and tense.

As he took off his topcoat and as she shut the front door, she said, "It was on the radio just now. The patrol officer ... the one who was shot ... he's – he's dead."

Anson walked into the sitting-room. He stood by the fire warming his cold hands. He watched her as she stood in the doorway, her cobalt-blue eyes sick with fear.

"Well?"

"Didn't you hear what I said?" she demanded, her voice shrill. "He is dead."

Anson peered at her. Again he was surprised how calm he felt. The fool had asked for it. He could have lived but he had asked for it. Now there was no reason to turn back ... Barlowe would be next. The cop's death sealed Barlowe's fate.

"What's the matter?" he asked.

"You shot him, didn't you?"

He looked around the room. She really was a slut, he thought as he saw the used breakfast things on the table. One of them, Barlowe of course, had had eggs and bacon. The yolk-encrusted plate, the smear of jam on the tablecloth, the used coffee cups by her typewriter disgusted him.

She stood watching him as he opened his briefcase and took out the gun. He wiped it carefully with his handkerchief and carrying it in his handkerchief, he put it in the wooden box he took from the drawer in the sideboard. He took five cartridges from his pocket, carefully wiped each one before putting them in the box.

"You've cleaned the gun?" she asked in a tight frightened voice.

"Of course."

"But you took six cartridges."

51

"Do you think he will miss one?" Anson asked, turning to look at her.

She shuddered.

"So you did kill that man ..."

He took hold of her wrist and jerked her roughly to him. "This is the beginning," he said, his hand sliding down the length of her back. She stiffened and tried to pull away from him, but he held her. "You said we would go ahead with this." His grip tightened. "Kiss me," he said urgently. "You're in this mess with me. You can't escape from it now. Kiss me."

She hesitated, then closing her eyes, she relaxed against him. As his lips met hers, he felt her shudder. Roughly he moved her around the settee, pushed her down so she lay on her back, staring up at him.

She shook her head wildly.

"No ... not now ... John! No!"

Seeing his sudden change of expression, an expression that frightened her, she pressed the palms of her hands against her eyes and shudderingly yielded to him.

"Tell me about yourself, Meg," Anson said some twenty minutes later. He was now sitting before the fire in the big shabby armchair while Meg still lay upon the settee. "You mustn't mind if I seem curious. I want you to be careful how you answer my questions. What I'm aiming to do is to make sure you don't land up in the gas chamber."

Meg moved uneasily.

"Why talk like that? You frighten me."

"It's better to be frightened by me than by Maddox," Anson said. "When eventually you put in the claim for the insurance money, Maddox will turn a searchlight on you. Even if you have a cast-iron alibi, he'll still be suspicious of you. Is there anything in your past he shouldn't know about?"

She frowned, not looking at him. "No ... of course not!"

"You have no criminal record?" She half sat up, her eyes angry.

"No!"

"You have never been in trouble with the police?"

She hesitated, then shrugging, she said, "Driving too fast ... that's all."

"What did you do before you were married?"

"I was a receptionist at an hotel."

"What hotel?"

"The Connaught Arms in Los Angeles."

"Was it a respectable hotel? It wasn't a room by the hour and no questions asked?"

"Of course not!"

"Before that?"

Again she hesitated before saying, "I was a night club hostess."

Anson became alert.

"What did you do?"

"The usual thing; partnered men, persuaded them to buy drinks."

"Now watch this, Meg. Did you go home with them? You know what I mean."

"I didn't."

He studied her. Her eyes were now angry.

"Sure?"

"I tell you I didn't!" She was now sitting bolt upright. "Is this man going to ask me these kind of questions before he'll pay out?"

Anson shook his head.

"Oh, no. But if he doesn't like the look of your claim, he'll turn one of his smart investigators on to you. Without your knowing anything about it, he'll dig up your whole history. He'll then decide when he has your dossier in front of him if he'll fight your claim or not. If your dossier is bad, he'll fight you."

She lay back, her expression showing how worried she was.

"If I'd known it was going to be like this, I wouldn't have agreed to do it with you."

"There's still time to back out," Anson said. "You can't expect to pick up fifty thousand dollars for nothing. You have nothing to worry about so long as you are telling the truth. What did you do before you became a night club hostess?"

"I lived with my mother," she said, not looking at him.

"You have been married nearly a year. This is vitally important, Meg. I must have the truth. While you have been Barlowe's wife, have you had a lover?"

"I've had you," Meg said and made a face at him.

"I don't mean me," Anson said, staring at her. "We've been careful, and we're going to remain careful. I mean someone else ... someone you haven't been so careful about."

"No ... there's been no one."

"Sure? If Maddox finds there has been someone, he'll go after him. There's nothing he likes better than to find out the wife of the insured husband who suddenly dies has a lover. He thrives on a situation like that."

"There's been no one."

"Would there be anyone who would know how you really feel about your husband? Anyone who might have overheard you quarrelling if you do quarrel? Anyone who might say you weren't happily married?"

She shook her head.

"No one ever comes here."

"Would your husband discuss you with anyone?"

She shook her head emphatically.

"No ... I'm sure of that."

Anson leaned back in the chair and thought for a long moment while Meg watched him.

"Okay," he said finally. "I think that covers it. You're sure you've told me the truth? You may not think so now, but all these questions are important. Once Maddox investigates you, and you can bet your life that's what he will do, you have to be above reproach. You are sure you have told me the truth?"

"Yes ... don't keep on and on! I have told you the truth!"

"Okay." He relaxed and took out a packet of cigarettes. He tossed her one and took one himself. As they lit up, he went on, "Now for the next step. Will your husband be home tomorrow night?"

"He's always home except on Mondays and Thursdays."

"I'll be here around eight thirty. Make sure you answer the door. I've got to get into this room if I'm to sell him. If he comes to the door, he may keep me on the doorstep and you don't sell insurance on a doorstep."

"Don't think you are going to have an easy time with Phil ... you won't."

Anson got to his feet.

"Your job is to open the front door and let me in. I'll do the rest. Tomorrow night then."

She stood up.

"John ... I want to know ... did you shoot that policeman?"

55

Anson picked up his briefcase.

"I told you not to ask questions." He paused and looked directly at her. "I have the money to pay for the premium ... that's all you need know."

He made no attempt to kiss her, but went out of the house and down the drive to his car.

As soon as the sound of his car engine had died away, Meg ran to the telephone and hurriedly dialled a number. She listened to the ringing tone for a long time, but there was no answer.

The following night was warm and mild with a brilliant moon. As things turned out this was lucky for Anson.

Meg had warned him Barlowe would be difficult but he hadn't imagined he was going to be as difficult as he was. Like most weak-willed people, Barlowe was not only obstinate; he was also rude.

Anson had no difficulty in getting in to the big sitting-room because Meg let him in, but when Barlowe jumped up from the armchair before the fire, an evening newspaper in his hand, Anson immediately felt the impact of hostility that came from the small ill-tempered looking man.

In spite of the hostility, Anson went smoothly into his usual sales talk, but he had scarcely begun, before Barlowe curtly cut him short.

"I'm not interested in insurance. I never have been and I never will be," he said. "You're wasting your time and mine. I'll be glad if you'll go."

Anson had smiled his friendly professional smile.

"I've come all the way from Brent, Mr Barlowe, to see you. I would take it as a favour if you would listen to what I have to say. I ..."

"I don't intend to listen!" Barlowe turned angrily to Meg who was standing in the doorway. "Why did you let him in? You know I never talk to salesmen!"

He sat down and opening his paper, he hid himself behind it.

Anson and Meg exchanged glances. She lifted her shoulders as if to say "Well, I told you, didn't I?"

To Anson this was a challenge. He was one of the top salesmen of the National Fidelity's group of salesmen. Over the years, he had often met with the complete brush-off and had survived to make a sale.

He said to the newspaper, hiding Barlowe, "Of course if I am annoying you I'll go, but I was under the impression you were interested in taking out a life policy. In fact, I was told to call on you."

Barlowe lowered the newspaper and stared suspiciously at Anson.

"Told? What do you mean? Who told you?"

Anson made an apologetic gesture.

"Mr Hammerstein," he said naming the general manager of Framley's store. He felt safe in using Hammerstein's name. In his lowly position as salesman, Barlowe wasn't likely to have contact with a man in Hammerstein's position. "I sold him a life policy and he said it would be a good idea if I called on some members of his staff. He gave me your name."

Barlowe flushed red.

"Mr Hammerstein gave you my name?"

"That's right," Anson said and smiled. "He seems to think a lot of you."

There was a pause, then Barlowe said in a milder tone, "I'm not interested. Anyway, thanks for calling."

"That's all right," Anson said. "I'm glad to have met you. I won't disturb you any longer."

Barlowe got hastily to his feet. He was now looking embarrassed.

"I didn't mean to seem rude," he said. "I wouldn't like you to think ... I mean ... well, one does get so pestered ..."

Anson's smile widened. This ill-tempered little man was now obviously scared word might get back to his boss that he had given Anson the brush-off.

"I know ... I know," he said. "Believe it or not some optimist the other day actually tried to sell me an insurance policy," and he laughed.

Barlowe laughed too. He was now losing his hostility and he moved forward as if to show Anson to the front door.

"I'll bet he didn't sell you anything," he said.

"And you wouldn't lose," Anson returned and laughed again.

Barlowe was now in the hall. With a quick wink at Meg, Anson joined him.

"I was admiring your garden," he said. "I would very much like to see it in daylight. As I drove up, my headlights showed me some of the finest roses I have ever seen."

Barlowe was about to open the front door; now he paused.

"Are you interested in gardening?"

"I'm crazy about it, but unfortunately I live in an apartment. My father had a cottage in Carmel. He grew roses, but they weren't in the same class as yours."

"Is that a fact?" Barlowe was now completely relaxed. "Would you like to see my garden?" His ill-tempered face softened. "I'll show it to you."

He opened a cupboard by the front door and Anson saw the cupboard contained a number of electrical switches.

Barlowe flicked them all down, then he opened the front door.

Anson moved forward, then paused.

The small garden had been transformed into a fairyland. Although he could see no sign of any lamps, the garden was now artistically and beautifully floodlit. It was as if the flowers themselves were producing their own lights. Even the fountain and the fish pond were bathed in blue and yellow lights.

"Well for Pete's sake!" Anson said, catching his breath. He pushed past Barlowe and stood on the drive, staring. There was no need for him to pretend. The sight of this beauty, the gay play of the fountain, the colour and the flowers caught him by the throat.

"I did it all," Barlowe said, standing by his side. "Everything ... I grew the flowers: lighted them: made the fountain ... I did everything."

"I would give five years of my life to be able to create a thing like that," Anson said and at that moment he meant it.

"I've given a lot of the years of my life learning how to do it," Barlowe said, and suddenly his face became pinched and ill-tempered again. "And where's it got me? Just a small-time job with Framley's."

Here it is, Anson thought. Here's what I've been waiting for! Turning to Barlowe, a look of puzzled astonishment on his face, he said, "But why work for anyone, Mr Barlowe, when you have such a talent? You could make a whale of a lot of money as a landscape architect."

Barlowe made an angry gesture.

"Do you think I haven't thought of that? How can I, without capital? I can't take risks. I'm married and I haven't anything behind me."

"Nothing behind you?" Anson said his voice incredulous. "That's ridiculous! You have this!" He waved dramatically towards the garden. "Any bank would advance you money if they saw this! Haven't you talked to them?"

"My bank won't advance me anything!" Barlowe said bitterly. "I've no security to offer. I have a minus credit rating. My mother cost me ... well, that's neither here nor there. I can't raise a loan. Even the house is mortgaged to the hilt!"

Anson walked away from him. He stood over the floodlit fish pond, watching the goldfish as they moved in the lighted water. He stood there for some moments before Barlowe joined him.

"This interests me," Anson said. "When I see a garden like this ... well, it excites me." He looked at Barlowe. "I see endless possibilities. How much capital would you need to start up on your own? I'm in touch with a lot of people in Brent, Lambsville and Pru Town ... wealthy people. They would be crazy to have a garden like this. I could give you a flock of introductions. How much capital do you want?"

Barlowe's face was suddenly alert and hopeful.

"What are we standing out here for?" he said, putting his hand on Anson's arm. "Let's go inside and I'll tell you about it."

As Anson re-entered the sitting-room and sat down on the settee, he gave Meg a quick furtive wink of triumph.

"I'll be working late, Anna," Anson said. "I have a policy to cope with. No need for you to hang around."

"I'll do it if you like, Mr Anson," Anna said, "I don't expect it will take long."

"It could do. Isn't this the night you take your boyfriend to the movies?"

Anna giggled.

"He takes me, you mean."

"Go on ... get off. I've nothing to do."

When she had gone, Anson went to the store cupboard and took from it four policy blanks. He put them on his desk, then lighting a cigarette, he leaned back in his desk chair.

It was now five days since he had talked Barlowe into taking out a $5,000 life insurance policy. Before the deal could be completed, Barlowe had to take the usual insurance medical examination. It would have been tough luck if he had failed it, but he hadn't. Dr Stevens, who acted for the National Fidelity, had said Barlowe was a first class life.

It was when Anson had explained to Barlowe how he could use a life policy to raise the capital he needed to set up as a horticultural architect – a phrase Anson kept using and which obviously pleased Barlowe – that Barlowe's sales resistance had disappeared. He had become so eager to sign that Anson was worried he had oversold his prospect. He had to explain to Barlowe that before the National Fidelity would accept him as a client he would have to pass a medical examination.

"The great advantage of this policy so far as you are concerned," Anson said hurrying over the sudden pause that followed when he had mentioned the medical examination, "is that you will be able to ask your bank manager, a year from signature, for three thousand dollars and get it without any fuss. You will only have to pay $150 to gain this advantage."

Barlowe frowned. He picked at the dirty adhesive bandage on his hand.

"Do you mean I have to wait a year before I can raise the capital I want?" he demanded. "Why, I thought ..."

"Excuse me, Mr Barlowe, but not so many minutes ago you told me you hadn't a hope of ever raising any kind of capital," Anson said quietly. "Now, in a year's time, because of this policy, you will be able to buy your land and start up in business."

Barlowe hesitated, then nodded.

"Yes ... all right. So what happens now?"

"As soon as I have the doctor's report, I'll come out with the policy for your signature," Anson said.

There was one final touch necessary to complete his plan.

"If you care to pay the first premium in cash, I'll be able to give you a five per cent discount. You may as well have the discount and it saves bookkeeping for me."

And of course Barlowe had agreed.

Anson picked up one of the policy blanks. He inserted it into the typewriter and filled in the necessary details. This policy was for $5,000: the beneficiary in the event of the death of the insured was to be Mrs Philip Barlowe.

He put in another blank, duplicating what he had already done. The third and fourth policy blanks were different. These, he made out for the sum of $50,000. If Barlowe happened to spot the difference, Anson could always say it was a typist's error.

Tomorrow night would be Thursday. Anson knew Meg would be alone. Although he was tempted to go out to the lonely house and make love to her, he knew this now would be too dangerous. He would have to wait. In six months, perhaps less, he and she would be together for as long as he liked: he and she and fifty thousand dollars ... worth waiting for.

He called the Barlowe house. Meg answered the telephone.

"It's all fixed," he said. "I'll be coming out the night after tomorrow. I told you I'd fix it, didn't I?"

"You are sure it is going to be all right?" The note of anxiety in her voice excited him. "When he has signed ... what are you going to do?"

"Let's wait until he signs," Anson said. "I'm thinking of you. I wish I were with you," and he put down the receiver.

A few minutes after six o'clock a.m. Philip Barlowe came awake with a sudden start. He had been dreaming. His grey-white pillow was damp with sweat.

He came awake the way an animal comes awake: instantly alert, suspicious, slightly frightened. He lay still, listening, then when he heard no sound to alarm him, he relaxed and moved further down in the single bed, making himself more comfortable.

Thursday!

The two days that meant more to him were Monday and Thursday when he got away from the house to spend the night alone after the dreary night classes when he attempted to instil into the minds of a group of pimply youths the basic theory of horticulture.

This night, he told himself, he would go out to Jason's Glen. There, he would be sure to find a number of smoochers and petters: young people behaving disgracefully in their second-hand cars. The thought of what he had heard and seen in the past brought beads of sweat out on his high forehead.

One of these days, he told himself, his small, well-shaped hands turning into fists, he would teach these sluts a lesson.

Their feeble, immoral petting disgusted him. Sometime in the very near future, some girl would learn what it meant to go beyond a giggle, a struggle and vapid gasp of breath.

Impatiently, he tossed off the blanket and sheet and got out of bed. He crossed to the mirror above the dressing-table and stared at himself. The shock of black hair, the white drawn ill-tempered face made him grimace. He turned away and walked over to a cupboard on the wall. He hesitated, listened, then took a key from his pyjama pocket. He unlocked the cupboard and looked at the .38 automatic revolver that lay on the shelf. By the gun was a white bathing cap. He picked up the cap; stretching it, he drew it down over his head. From the shelf he took two small rubber pads. These he fitted between his gums and the inside of his cheeks ... they filled out his face, altering his appearance in a startling way. He moved over to the mirror and stared again at himself. The ill-tempered, thin-faced Barlowe had disappeared. Instead, there was a fat-faced nightmarish looking creature, the white bathing cap making him look completely bald. He picked up the gun. His fingers curled lovingly around the trigger, and he smiled.

Not so far in the future, he told himself, this gun would explode into sound. Not so far into the future ... someone would die.

He put the gun back on to the shelf. He took off the bathing cap. He took the rubber pads from his mouth and replaced them on the shelf. Then he carefully locked the cupboard door. He paused for a long moment staring into space, then whistling tunelessly, he went into the bathroom.

Twenty minutes later, he returned to his room. He dressed, again opened the cupboard and put the bathing cap and the rubber pads into his hip pocket. For a long moment he stared at the gun, hesitated then decided to leave it where it was.

He stepped into the corridor. He paused outside Meg's bedroom door. He put his ear against the locked door panel and listened. He could hear nothing. He stood there for several moments, then with a frustrated grimace, he went down the stairs to prepare his routine breakfast of eggs and bacon.

Unaware of what had been going on, Meg continued to sleep restlessly.

Jason's Glen was a favourite place for young couples who were lucky enough to have a car, but unfortunate enough to have no room, little money, and no facilities in which to make love. No matter what the weather offered, Jason's Glen always had at least two or three cars in which couples made desperate and natural love.

This Thursday night, rain was falling. There were only two cars parked under the trees. One of them was a small British sports car: the other a battered, aged Buick.

From under the heavy overgrown shrubs, Barlowe watched the two cars. They were separated by some fifty yards.

Suddenly a girl exclaimed: "Jeff! No! What do you think you're doing? Jeff! ... No!"

The voice came from the Buick.

Crouching like a black crab, the white bathing helmet pulled down over his thick black hair, Barlowe crept out into the rain towards the parked Buick.

The man in the sports car called out, "Don't let her take no for an answer, pal," and the girl with him gave a squeal of hysterical laughter.

Barlowe suddenly had a furious, frustrated desire to have his gun in his hand. With a gun ... he could teach these young, filthy animals a lesson.

He moved up to the Buick, unaware of the rain that was beating down on his crouched body. When the girl in the car began to moan, Barlowe suddenly fell on his knees. His hands clawed into the wet, soft soil. He remained like that, his body arched, and when the girl suddenly cried out, he dug his fingers deeper into the soil.

Anson was flicking through a pile of coupon inquiries when the telephone bell rang.

Anna picked up the receiver.

Looking across at her from his desk, Anson saw her usual placid expression change to alertness and he had a sudden feeling of danger.

"Yes ... yes, he's here. I'll put you through." Anna looked at Anson and waved the telephone receiver warningly. Then she flicked down the key and hissed, "It's Mr Maddox."

His face wooden, his heart suddenly thumping, Anson picked up his receiver and said, "Anson here."

A hard, curt voice barked, "I want you out here. How are you fixed for tomorrow?"

"I can manage that," Anson said, "anything special?"

"You don't imagine I'd pull you off your territory just to look at you, do you?" Maddox snapped. "Okay, then ten o'clock tomorrow," and he hung up.

Anson replaced his receiver, pushed back his chair and walked to the window so Anna couldn't see how white he had gone.

Barlowe's policy for $50,000, signed and completed, had gone to Head Office three days ago. Why had Maddox got on to it so quickly? Anson dug his sweating hands into his trouser pockets as he wondered.

"What does he want?" Anna asked curiously. Making an effort, Anson returned to his desk. He sat down.

"I don't know," he said, picking up another batch of coupons. "Why should I worry?"

Anna lifted her fat shoulders.

"Well, if you're not worrying, why should I?" Anson went on sorting through the coupons. There was a chill around his heart. Maddox! Even before Barlowe was dead this jinx of a man was suspicious ... or was he?

Anson lit a cigarette. Better now than after Barlowe was dead. If it looked too dangerous, he wouldn't go ahead with his plan. It was better now to know the worst before he was so far out on a limb he couldn't scramble back.

Maddox!

5

Patty Shaw, Maddox's secretary, was typing busily when Anson entered the small outer office.

She looked up, took her hands off the keys and smiled a welcome.

"Hello, John, nice to see you again. How's it out in the back of the beyond?"

Anson returned her smile. All the National Fidelity salesmen were fond of Patty: apart from her blonde prettiness, she was smart and helpful. She understood a salesman's difficulties and she knew how discouraging Maddox could be.

"Not so bad. What's he want?" Anson jerked his head to the door that led into Maddox's office.

"The Vodex car smash," Patty said, rolling her blue eyes. "He's trying to get out of paying the claim. He wants your angle on it."

Anson drew in a long, slow breath of relief. And he had been thinking it was the Barlowe policy Maddox was going to gripe about.

"He can't get out of paying it!" he exclaimed angrily. "What's the matter with the man? Vodex was drunker than a skunk! We've got to pay!"

"You know how he is," Patty said, lifting her shoulders.

"He'll try anything to get out of paying a claim." She flicked down a key on her intercom. "Mr Anson's here, Mr Maddox."

A hard curt voice barked, "Shoot him right in."

"Go ahead," Patty said, waving to the door. "Remember Daniel in the lion's den. Daniel didn't give a damn for the lions, and the lions didn't give a damn for Daniel."

Anson forced a grin and then went into Maddox's office.

Maddox was sitting behind a vast desk, smothered in papers. There were papers on the floor, papers on most of the chairs and papers everywhere.

Maddox was glaring at a policy he held in his thick freckled fingers. His thinning grey hair was rumpled and his red face was screwed into a scowl. Maddox wasn't a big man although he looked big from behind the shelter of his desk. He had the shoulders of a boxer and the legs of a midget. His eyes were restless, alert and bleak. He wore his well-cut clothes anyhow. Cigarette ash rained on his sleeves, his tie and his lap. He had a habit of running his stubby fingers constantly through his hair which added to his dishevelled appearance.

He leaned back in the chair and glared at Anson.

"Well, come on in," he said. "Sit down. This sonofabitch, Vodex ..." and as Anson sat down, Maddox launched into a steady invective against their client.

Twenty minutes later, Maddox made a gesture of disgust and reached for another cigarette.

"Okay, so we'll have to pay up! Forty thousand dollars! You salesmen kill me! Couldn't you have seen this jerk was an alcoholic? All you think about is your commission! If you had a grain of insight, we'd be forty thousand dollars in pocket!"

69

"It's my job to sell insurance," Anson said sharply. "You don't have to beef to me. If you have any complaint take it up with Doc Stevens. He okayed Vodex. If you don't like the way I sell insurance you'd better talk to Mr Burrows."

Burrows was the President of the National Fidelity, the only man who could talk back to Maddox.

Maddox lit another cigarette.

"Okay, okay," he said, waving his stubby hands. "Don't get your shirt out. But this kills me! Forty thousand dollars! What's the matter with Stevens? Doesn't he know a drunk when he sees one?"

"Vodex wasn't a drunk!" Anson said patiently. "He happened to be drunk on the night of the crash. He hasn't been drunk in years."

Maddox shrugged and suddenly relaxed. His red, rubbery face contorted into a sour grin.

"Well, let's forget it. How's business Anson? How are you doing?"

Knowing his man, Anson wasn't fooled. Cautiously he said, "It's all right. This is a bad month. I have a number of prospects lined up once they have paid their rents and bills."

"You're not doing so bad," Maddox said and dived into a mass of papers on his desk. He came up with a policy which he studied, then looked at Anson with a sudden cold penetrating stare.

"What's this? This guy Barlowe? You hooked him for fifty thousand dollars?"

Anson's face was expressionless as he said, "Oh Barlowe ... yes, that was a lucky one. He sent in a coupon inquiry and I nailed him."

"Fifty thousand, huh?" Maddox stared at the policy, then dropped it on his desk. "Who is Barlowe?"

"Probably one of the best gardeners I've ever come across," Anson said. "He works in the horticultural department of Framley's stores. I don't know if you are interested in gardening, but he has the finest small garden I've ever seen."

"I'm not interested in anything except the work that lies under my nose and the pen I hold in my hand," Maddox misquoted sourly. "So this guy works at Framley's stores, does he? How come he can afford a policy this size?"

"He wants to use it to raise capital to buy himself a business," Anson said. "After a couple of years, he'll ask us to pay the premiums out of the policy."

"Nice for him," Maddox said scowling. "In the meantime if he happens to drop dead, we're in the hole for fifty thousand bucks."

"Stevens rates him as a first class life."

"That quack! He can't even recognise a drunk when he sees one!"

Anson didn't say anything. He watched Maddox light yet another cigarette.

"The beneficiary is Mrs Barlowe ... that his wife?"

"Yes." Anson felt his heart give a little kick against his side.

"What's she like?" Maddox asked, staring at Anson.

"You mean what does she look like?" Anson asked, his voice casual, his expression inquiring.

"Yeah ... I like to have a picture of people in my mind," Maddox said. "When I get a policy for this amount come out of the blue and I learn the insured is just a counter clerk, I get interested. What's she like?"

"Attractive, around twenty-seven. I didn't talk to her much. I talked to Barlowe. I got the impression they were happy together," Anson said carefully.

Maddox picked up the policy and stared at it. "How come this guy pays the first premium in cash?" he asked.

"He wanted it that way. He keeps money in his house. Anything wrong about it?"

Maddox grimaced.

"I don't know. Twelve hundred is a lot of dough to keep in your house. Hasn't he a banking account?"

"I guess so. I didn't ask him."

Maddox blew a stream of tobacco smoke down his thick nostrils. His red rubbery face was screwed up in an expression of thought.

"So he wants to use this policy to raise capital ... that it?"

"That's what he told me."

"To set up as a gardener?"

"Well, more than that ... to buy land, greenhouses, machines and so on."

"How much capital does he want?"

Anson shrugged.

"I don't know. I didn't ask him. He said he wanted to insure his life and he told me why. I didn't argue with him."

"That's right," Maddox said and put the policy down on his desk. "So long as you make a sale, you don't have to worry, do you?"

"It's my job to make a sale," Anson said quietly. "That's what I get paid for." He stood up. "Is there anything else?"

"No, I guess that's about it," Maddox said, without looking at Anson.

"Then I'll get back. Will see you."

Maddox nodded absently. He still didn't look at Anson. He was staring at the Barlowe policy. He was still staring at it, lost in thought, several minutes after Anson had gone. Then, suddenly coming to life, he flicked down a key on the intercom and said, "Harmas around?"

"Yes, Mr Maddox," Patty said. "I'll call him."

Three minutes later, Steve Harmas, Maddox's chief investigator, wandered in. He was a tall broad-shouldered man; dark around thirty-three with a deeply tanned ugly but humorous face. He had married Maddox's favourite secretary, something that Maddox had never got over, but as Harmas was by far his best investigator, Maddox had been forced to accept the fact.

"You wanted me?" Harmas asked as he folded his long lean body into the client's chair.

Maddox tossed him the Barlowe policy.

"Look at that," he said, then spilling ash over his papers, he selected yet another policy and began to examine it suspiciously.

Harmas looked through the policy handed to him, then he put it on the desk.

"Nice work," he said. "Anson is a smart cookie."

Maddox bent his chair back until it creaked under the weight of his massive shoulders.

"I'm not so sure he is so smart," he said. "Take this policy. Barlowe is a ten-a-dime salesman at Framley's stores, Pru Town. What's he doing taking out a life policy for fifty thousand dollars?"

Harmas shrugged.

"I don't know ... you tell me."

"I'd like to," Maddox said. "If Barlowe suddenly drops dead, we're in the hole for fifty thousand bucks. The story is he has taken out this policy so he can raise enough capital to set up as a gardener. What would he want fifty thousand for to set up as a gardener?"

Harmas scratched the back of his neck. He knew Maddox. He knew Maddox wasn't asking for information. He was talking to himself.

"Go ahead ... I'm here to listen," he said.

"That's about all you're good for," Maddox said bitterly. "I have hunches. I don't like this policy. I have a hunch about it. It gives off a smell."

Harmas grinned.

"Is there any policy that comes to you that doesn't give off a smell?"

"A few do ... but not many. Here's what you do. I want to know everything there is to know about Barlowe and his wife: repeat his wife. Get a Tracing Agency on to them and have them send everything they can dig up direct to me. Understand?"

"Okay," Harmas said, getting to his feet. "If that's what you want, that's what you'll get."

"Why didn't this guy take out a five thousand dollar insurance?" Maddox asked. "Why fifty thousand? Why did he pay the first premium in cash?"

"I wouldn't know," Harmas said, "but if you're all that interested, I guess I'll have to find out."

Maddox nodded.

"That's it ... find out," and reaching for another policy, he settled down to examine it.

Late back from his trip to San Francisco, Anson was thinking about going to bed when his door bell rang. Wondering who could be calling at this hour, he went to the door.

A woman, wearing a black coat and a green and yellow scarf over her head, hiding her face, moved quickly past him into the room.

"Shut the door!" she said sharply.

"Meg!"

Anson hurriedly shut and locked the door as Meg Barlowe took off the scarf.

"What are you doing here?" Anson asked, alarmed.

"I had to come." She took off her coat and tossed it on a chair. "I've been trying to contact you all day."

"Did anyone see you come in?" Anson asked. "Don't you realise if we are seen together ..."

"I was careful. No one saw me. Anyway, even if they did see me they wouldn't recognise me." She came over to him and slid her arms around him. "Aren't you pleased to see me?"

The feel of her body as she pressed herself against him lessened Anson's alarm. He kissed her with mounting passion until she broke away.

"Where have you been?" she asked, moving away and sitting on the arm of an armchair. "I tried to telephone you."

"I've just got back from Frisco," Anson said. "Look, Meg, I warned you we have to be careful. You must never telephone me. Our plan stands or falls on the fact that we are practically strangers. You must understand that!"

She made an impatient movement.

"What's been happening?"

He told her about his interview with Maddox. She listened, her cobalt-blue eyes worried.

"There's nothing to be worried about," he said. "Maddox won't take it further. He's satisfied."

She looked down at her hands as she asked, "When do you ... get rid of Phil?"

"Not yet. We must wait. Four or five months at least."

She stiffened.

"Four or five *months*!"

"Yes. If we don't wait, we'll be in trouble. Imagine how Maddox would react if your husband died within a few weeks of insuring himself. It'll be bad enough if he dies in four or five months' time, but sooner than that would be out of the question."

"How will you do it?"

The intensity of her stare began to irritate him.

"I don't know. I haven't even thought about it yet. This idea I had of him falling and drowning in the pond won't work. I couldn't be sure someone might come up the road while I was fixing it. It'll have to happen in the house."

Meg shivered.

"But how?"

"I don't know. I have to think about it. When I get the right idea, I'll tell you."

"But must we really wait all that time?"

"If we rush this, we could ruin everything. Isn't fifty thousand dollars worth waiting for?"

She hesitated, then nodded.

"Yes, of course." She paused, then went on, "so you have no idea how you'll do it?"

"Don't keep on and on," Anson said impatiently. "At least I have him now insured for fifty thousand dollars and that's something you didn't think I could fix."

"Yes ... you were clever about that." She stood up. "I must go," and she picked up her coat.

"Go?" Anson's face became tense, "but why? Now you're here ... he's not going home tonight, is he? Of course you must stay ..."

"I can't." She slipped on her coat and began to put the scarf on her head. "I promised I would go to his class tonight. That's why I'm here. He drove me down this morning. I've been trying to get you all day."

76

He made to take her in his arms, but she avoided him.

"No, John, I must go."

"Then when do we have a few minutes together?" he demanded, his voice edged with frustration. "Now you're here: oh, come on, Meg ... I want you ..."

"No! I have to go! I shouldn't have come here. I have to go!"

The sudden hardness in her eyes warned him it would be useless to attempt to persuade her to stay.

"You can kiss me, can't you?" he said angrily.

She let him kiss her, but when he became ardent, she pushed him roughly away.

"I said no!"

His face congested, his eyes sullen with frustrated anger, Anson went to the front door, opened it and looked out on to the deserted corridor.

"I'll call you," he said as she moved past him.

He listened to her heels click on the stairs as she went down the street.

A dusty 1958 Buick was parked at the end of the street in which Anson's apartment block stood.

Sailor Hogan sat at the wheel, a cigarette dangling from his lips, his big hands resting on his knees. His hard eyes moved continuously to his driving mirror to check the street behind him and then through the windshield to check the street ahead of him.

When he saw Meg come out of Anson's apartment block, he started the car engine. As Meg reached the car, he leaned across the bench seat and swung open the door. Meg slid in, slammed the door as Hogan shot the car away from the kerb.

"Well? What did he say?" Hogan demanded.

"At least four or five months," Meg told him and flinched away from the explosion she knew would follow.

"*Months*?" Hogan's voice shot up. "You crazy? You mean weeks, don't you?"

"He said months. He says they'll be suspicious if he does it before."

"I don't give a damn what he says!" Hogan snarled. "It's got to happen before then! I can't wait that long! I must have the money by the end of the month!"

"If you think you can do better than me ... then you talk to him," said Meg sullenly.

Hogan gave her a quick vicious glance.

"Okay, baby," he said. "We'll see about this."

He shoved his foot down on the gas pedal and the car surged forward.

Neither of them spoke until they reached the Barlowe house. Meg got out of the car and opened the double gates. Hogan drove the car into the garage. He joined Meg as she unlocked the front door. They walked side by side into the dark house and into the sitting-room.

When Meg had lowered the blinds, she turned on the lights.

Hogan stood over the fire, his big hands thrust into his pockets while he watched Meg get a bottle of whisky and glasses from the cupboard.

Hogan was above middle height with the wide muscular shoulders of a boxer. He wore his wavy, dark hair cut short. He was handsome in a brutish way. During his professional fighting career his nose had been flattened. There were scar tissues along the ridge of his eyebrows, but this added to rather than detracted from his animal glamour.

"Listen, doll," he said, "you've got to do better than this." He took the glass half full of whisky Meg handed to him. "I've got to have this money by the end of the month! You've got to talk this guy into doing his stuff by then or you and me will fall out."

Meg sat on the settee. She was pale and her eyes were anxious.

"It's no use, Jerry," she said. "You don't know him the way I do. He scares me." She shivered. "I can't handle him. I wish I hadn't listened to you! I wish ..."

"Aw, shut up!" Hogan snarled. "You do what I tell you or I'll give you something to remember me by!"

Meg looked at him.

"That policeman who was shot at the Caltex hold-up ... Anson did it."

Hogan stiffened.

"Anson? You're lying, you rotten little ..."

"He did it!" Meg exclaimed, jumping to her feet and backing away as Hogan, his hands now out of his pockets began to move threateningly towards her. "He killed him with Phil's gun!"

Hogan paused, then he rubbed his jaw with a sweating hand.

"So that's how he raised the money!" he said startled. "Joe and me wondered how he had got it. Well! what do you know ... a cop killer!"

"It didn't mean a thing to him!" Meg exclaimed. "He's dangerous, Jerry. I'm warning you! Those eyes of his! He scares me. I wish you hadn't picked on him."

"I picked on the right guy," Hogan said. He finished the whisky and set down the glass. "It was your idea to get Barlowe insured, wasn't it? How else could we have worked it without having some punk in the insurance racket to fix it? Well, Anson's fixed it, hasn't he. He had to: I saw to that. With the money owing to Sam Bernstein and

79

me to put pressure on him, he was a natural." He sat down beside her. "Get me another drink. Phew! A cop killer!" As Meg came back with another glass half full of neat whisky, he asked, "Has he still got the gun?"

"No. He brought it back the next day. I've been trying to get you for days but you're never in."

Hogan made an impatient movement.

"If I'd known he was that tough, I'd been more careful how I handled him ... a cop killer!" He drank some of the whisky and blew out his cheeks. "Well, what are we going to do? I must have the money by the end of the month. This is a chance in a lifetime. Joe told me this morning he couldn't wait. There's another punk waiting to put up the money, but Joe wants me to be his partner. It's cheap at the price ... twenty-five grand and Joe won't ask questions."

"It's no good, Jerry. You'll have to wait."

Hogan stared into the fire for a long moment while Meg watched him anxiously.

"What's wrong with me knocking Phil off?" he asked suddenly. "He's insured now ... that was the tricky part. I could fix him and then we'd have the dough without having to wait for this punk Anson to make up his mind."

"No!" Meg's voice went shrill. "I won't let you! You must keep clear of this, Jerry! You must have a cast-iron alibi same as me! That's the whole trick in my plan to keep us both in the clear and let Anson take the blame if any thing goes wrong. You must keep out of this!"

"Well, we've got to do something!" Hogan snarled, suddenly angry again. "Stir yourself. I can't wait five months!"

"I'll think of something," Meg said desperately.

Hogan got to his feet.

"You'd better or I'll look elsewhere for the dough." He caught hold of her by the arms and shook her. "Listen, I'm getting sick of this! This was your great idea! Okay! ... make it work or you and me will part company! We've parted company before. You've got nothing another woman can't give me! Hear me! If we part this time ... we part for good!"

"I'll fix it!" Meg said desperately. "Honestly, Jerry ... I'll fix it!"

"You'd better!" He started towards the door, paused and glared at her. "And fix it fast!"

"You're not leaving, Jerry?" She looked pleadingly at him. "I haven't seen you for so long. He won't be back tonight ..."

Hogan's battered face twisted into a contemptuous sneer. "You imagine you've got something to keep me here?" he asked. "I've things to do. You fix Anson!"

She came to him, but he shoved her roughly away.

"Keep your paws off me! You use your head instead of your body for a change! I want the dough by the end of the month ... or you and me are through for good!"

He left the house, slamming the front door.

Meg stood motionless. It was not until the sound of his car had died away that she moved stiffly to the settee. She sat down. A convulsive sob shook her, but she quickly controlled herself. She picked up the bottle of whisky and poured herself a stiff shot. She had thought she had lost Hogan before, but he had come back. This time she could lose him for good if she didn't do something. The thought of losing him made her feel sick and weak. She drank the whisky and with a sudden desperate gesture, she threw the glass into the fire.

It was when the whisky began to move through her body, relaxing her, that Meg thought back to the time when she had first met Jerry Hogan. It seemed a long time to her, but it was only three years ... much had happened to her during these three years.

Then she had been a waitress in a small Hollywood restaurant. Hogan had come in with a short, fat elderly man named Benny Hirsch who she learned later was Hogan's fight manager.

Hogan had just lost his Californian light heavyweight title. He had been knocked out with a sucker punch in the first two minutes of the first round. Apart from an aching jaw, he was unscarred. Meg had no idea who he was. She had come to the table, her order pad in her hand and had looked indifferently at the two men.

Hogan had been in a vicious, frightened mood. His career, long threatened by his sexual excesses and his heavy drinking, had now blown up in his face. He could see Hirsch was no longer interested in him. There was plenty of young keen fighters who could keep Hirsch in the money without him having to bother with a beat-up, womaniser like Hogan, and Hogan knew it.

"A coffee," Hirsch said without looking at Hogan.

Hogan stared at him.

"A coffee? What the hell? Aren't you hungry? I want a steak."

Hirsch shifted around and looked him over, dislike and contempt on his fat face.

"Yeah ... you sure need a steak," he said bitterly. "I don't even need a coffee. The sight of you makes me sick to my stomach. Steak! Some fighter! You do your best fighting in bed with a bottle." He got to his feet. "I don't know why I even came here with you. You're through, Hogan. As far as

82

I am concerned, you're yesterday's smell of boiled cabbage!"

Startled and shocked, Meg watched Hirsch walk out of the restaurant. She then looked at Hogan who sat limply in his chair, sweat beads on his face, and at that moment, seeing him in defeat, she was stupid enough to fall in love with him. When the restaurant closed, Hogan went with her to her small bedroom above an unsuccessful dry-cleaning establishment. His fierce, brutal, selfish lovemaking was something Meg had never experienced. That first sordid act of so-called love chained her to this man, excusing his viciousness, his cowardice, his cheating and his drinking.

Early the following morning, Hogan came awake and looked at Meg, sleeping at his side. Here, he told himself was a meal ticket. He knew he was through with fighting. He had to live somehow, and this dish, with her looks, could at least keep him in food, drink and cigarettes.

It took him a few days to convince Meg that if she really wanted to have him as her lover, she would have to give up her job as a waitress and start hustling. Hogan made it easy for her. He went round to a couple of pimps who controlled a certain, profitable beat and told them his girl was moving in. They regarded him thoughtfully, remembered that he was an ex-light heavyweight, and decided it would be wise to offer no opposition.

For the next year, Meg worked the streets, giving her earnings willingly to Hogan who used the money either for backing horses or to finance himself in all-night poker games he and his fellow pimps arranged.

Then Meg began to realise the poker game was a blind. While she was working, Hogan was chasing other girls. The money she made he now was spending on any woman he happened to run into during the night hours Meg tramped her beat.

One night, returning drunk, with lipstick on his shirt, Hogan told her that they were parting company. Meg listened to his drunken slurring contempt, with fear clutching at her heart. Life without Hogan, no matter how he behaved, was unthinkable to her.

"You're chick-feed," Hogan had sneered. "I'm going to look for a girl who can earn big money ... not a run-down street floosie like you. You and me are through!"

The following afternoon, Meg was in the ladies' room of a smart hotel. She was about to go up to the fourth floor where a middle-aged businessman was impatiently waiting for her. By one of the toilet basins she saw an expensive lizard-skin bag. She stared at it, hesitated, then moving quickly, she opened it. The bag was stuffed with fifty-dollar bills. For a long moment she stared at the money, then grabbing the bills, she transferred them to her own handbag. Her one thought was that with this money, Hogan would remain with her.

As she moved to the door, the door opened. A woman and the hotel detective came in.

Hogan wasn't at the trial. Meg went away for three months, and when she came out, Hogan had vanished. She had no money, no protection and the police pestered her.

Finally, in desperation, she left Los Angeles and headed for San Francisco. Her money ran out when she got as far as Pru Town on a Greyhound bus. She managed to rent a small room on the top floor of an office block. It was her bad luck to strike the worst winter for the past fifty years. The newspapers made headlines about the frost, snow and cold. She had no pimp to protect her and she had no regular beat. It was when she was ill, frozen and defeated not caring what happened to her, using her last few dollars on cheap whisky, that she met Phil Barlowe.

She would always remember that moment when he came furtively out of the darkness. She was standing under a street lamp, wet snow falling on her, her feet frozen, aware that the cold had turned her face into a stiff white mask.

Barlowe, wearing a black, slouch hat and a dark topcoat, had paused and they looked at each other.

"Are you looking for a naughty girl?" Meg asked, her lips so stiff with the cold she had trouble in speaking.

"How naughty?"

The pale brown eyes scared her. The thin, ill-tempered face warned her this man could be a sadist, but she was beyond caring. She had to have money. If this mean looking creature had money, then she would take a chance with him.

They had gone together to her room. Barlowe had sat on one of the chairs making no attempt to take off his topcoat. Meg had sat listlessly on the bed, shivering.

"Come on, honey," she said impatiently, "don't just sit there."

"I only want to talk to you," Barlowe said. "I've got no one I can talk to."

She was so used to nuts, perverts and queers, that she wasn't surprised.

"Look, honey," she said. "It'll cost you either way. Let's have your present."

He fumblingly, produced his wallet and gave her three ten-dollar bills. Meg, who had been working for practically nothing, couldn't believe her eyes.

The room was heated by a small paraffin stove. It was enough only to keep out the frost. Cold, shivering and feeling she was now running a temperature, Meg pulled the blankets over her and settled down in the bed, fully dressed.

She half listened to Barlowe talking. She vaguely gathered his mother had just died and he was lonely. He talked on and on and on. She had an idea he told her he had money, a cottage and a lovely garden. She gathered sleepily that he had a good job in some store. Warmth at last began to steal over her and she fell asleep.

She woke the next morning to find the stove out, the window covered with white frost and her head aching wildly. Barlowe had gone. She sat up in panic and opened her handbag, but the thirty dollars was still there. She remained in bed, too ill to move, and at one time she thought she might be dying.

Sometime during the evening, as the shadows lengthened and the cold sordid little room began to dissolve into darkness, she heard a tapping on the door.

By then she was too ill to bother. She became aware vaguely that Barlowe was standing over her, his bitter distressed face close to hers. She tried to say something ... to tell him to go away, but the effort was too much for her. She grimaced and closed her eyes, sinking into a feverish, frightening oblivion.

Later, she was vaguely aware of being carried down the narrow stairs in a kind of hammock ... the stairs being so narrow and difficult a stretcher was impossible. She found herself in a hospital bed and she was in the quiet ward for ten days. Each day Barlowe came and sat by her side. He just stared at her and said nothing. She was so ill and weak she accepted him ... a nut ... but she was grateful for what he had done for her. During these ten days she constantly thought of Jerry Hogan, wondering where he was, who he was sleeping with, how he was making money enough to live.

Then suddenly, one morning, she woke up and she knew she was well again. Her one thought was to get out of the hospital, but she shrank from returning to that sordid room with its inadequate stove and the bitter wind that whistled under the door and through the cracks of the ill-fitting windows.

Barlowe came in the evening. They talked.

"I've been pretty ill," she said. "I don't know anything about you ... why have you been so kind?"

"It's not kindness," he said quietly, his pale brown eyes moving over her in a way that made her uneasy. "You and I are lonely people. I have a cottage: a garden: a good job. I've lost my mother. I'd like to marry you. Will you marry me?"

Right at that moment, thinking of the life that lay before her if she continued to try to battle along on her own, Meg didn't hesitate. She regarded marriage as a convenience. If it didn't work out, you could always get a divorce, so she accepted his offer.

They were married by a special licence a week after Meg had left hospital. She had been at first intrigued and pleased with the isolated house and the garden. She believed that she would be able to find some kind of happiness here, but she was quickly disillusioned.

She now never wanted to remember their first and only night together. It ended by Meg locking herself in the spare room while Barlowe scratched on the door as he knelt outside in the passage. She realised bitterly that she had married one of those sick minded men who she had had to cope with so often during the time she had walked her beat in Hollywood.

But she knew herself to be hard and ruthless enough to control this poor, sick little man. They lived their individual lives. Then, some months later, as she was shopping in Brent, she came face to face with Sailor Hogan.

The sight of his reckless, handsome face sent a knife stab into her heart. Less than an hour later, they were lying on his bed in his small two-room apartment and she was telling him about Barlowe.

They met frequently, and during the weeks, while they talked, after Hogan had made brutal love with her, the idea that Barlowe could bring them the money they craved for began to evolve.

Hogan knew an insurance agent. Meg thought of the idea of insuring Barlowe's life. Between the two of them they concocted the murder plan.

But now, as Meg, slightly drunk, sat on the settee staring into the fire, she realised that unless she came up with some bright idea, she would again lose Hogan. She sat there, her fists clenched between her knees, her mind active, her heart pounding with the sick thought of once again facing life without her brutal, vicious pimp.

6

Barlowe stood by his bedroom door, listening. The time was just after nine thirty. It was Sunday night. Downstairs, Meg was watching a television programme. He had told her he was tired and was going to bed early. She had shrugged indifferently.

Satisfied she was occupied with some pop singer who sounded to Barlowe like a banshee, he unlocked the cupboard on the wall, took from it the white bathing cap and the cheek pads, and with a fixed grin on his face, he picked up the .38 automatic, checked to see it was loaded, then dropped it into his overcoat pocket.

Moving stealthily, he left his bedroom, locking the door. He crept down the stairs, paused outside the sitting-room door to listen to the strident singing of the pop singer, then let himself out into the hot, still night.

He was afraid to use his car for he knew Meg would hear him drive away, so he set out for the long walk across country to Glyn Hill, yet another quiet, favourite place where the young made love in their cars.

He arrived at the open space that overlooked Pru Town a little after ten-fifteen. Moving like a black, sinister crab, he edged his way through the shrubs.

There was one lone car parked under the trees. It was early yet. In another hour, there would be several cars. From the lone car came the faint sound of dance music on the radio. Satisfied there was no one on this plateau except the two in the car, Barlowe took off his hat and pulled the white bathing cap down over his head. He then replaced his hat. He put the cheek pads into place, then taking the gun from his pocket, he began to move silently and swiftly towards the car.

His heart hammered, his breath came in short, snorting gasps ... this time, he was no longer going to be a mere onlooker; a mere peeping Tom.

On the following Monday morning as Anson was preparing to go to Pru Town, the telephone bell rang.

Anna answered the call, said, "Yes, he's here: who is it please?" Then to Anson, "A Mrs Thomson wants you," and she flicked down the key.

Impatiently, Anson scooped up his receiver.

"Yes? This is John Anson."

"John ... it is me."

With a feeling of shock, Anson recognised Meg's voice. He looked furtively across at Anna who was threading paper into her typewriter. Alarmed that Meg had been reckless enough to call him at his office, but excited to hear her voice again, he said "Yes, Mrs Thomson?"

"I must see you tonight. Something has happened."

Guardedly, Anson said, "I'll be able to manage that. Thank you for calling," and he hung up.

As Anna showed no interest in the call, Anson didn't bother to lie to her. He hurriedly completed his preparations. Telling Anna he would be back the following morning, he went down to his car.

During the day he kept thinking of Meg and wondering what had happened to make her call him. On his way to lunch at the Marlborough he stopped off at a drug store for some aftershave lotion. As he was paying for his purchase a woman who had come in after him, said, "Hello Johnny ... long time no see."

Turning sharply, he found Fay Lawley, the girl he used to go around with before he had dropped her for Meg, standing by his side.

Fay's coarse prettiness and her enthusiastic wantonness had once attracted Anson, but looking at her now, he marvelled that he had ever found her interesting.

"Hello, Fay," he said in a cold, flat voice. "Excuse me ... I'm pressed for time."

"See you tonight, Johnny?" Fay asked, staring at him, her eyes hard and challenging.

He forced a smile.

"I'm afraid not ... not tonight. I'll call you the next time in town."

Side stepping her, he made a move to the door, but she caught hold of his arm.

"Remember me?" Her eyes now granite hard, scared him. "You and me met once a week ... remember?"

He steeled himself and shook her off.

"Take it easy, Fay ... I just happen to be busy." He pushed past her and walked to his car. He was aware sweat was on his face and there was a hollow feeling of alarm around his heart.

He drove to the Marlborough, and parking his car, he entered the restaurant where he was joined by Harry Davis, an oil and gas salesman who he often met on the road.

Davis was a fat, middle-aged man who had the happy knack of getting along with anyone. But with this puzzle of what Meg had said on his mind, Anson would have preferred to have eaten alone.

91

After they had ordered the lunch, Davis asked Anson how business was. The two men discussed business conditions while they ate the excellent pea soup, then as the waiter brought them the fried chicken, Davis said, "I don't know what this town is coming to! Two shootings in ten days! We want a smarter police chief! We've got to stamp out this kind of violence and at once!"

Anson looked up sharply.

"Two shootings! What's this?"

"Haven't you seen this morning's newspaper?"

"No. What's all this?"

Happily, Davis relaxed back in his chair.

"A real juicy murder-cum-sex crime! A young couple were necking out at Glyn Hill last night when some maniac crept up on them with a gun. He shot the man and raped the girl. I knew the murdered man ... he had been going steady with the girl for the past six months. It's a hell of a thing! The girl was horribly used. Of course, the police haven't a clue. At least they have a description of the killer. This, and the Caltex murder must be making Jenson spin like a top."

"He's got nowhere with the Caltex shooting, has he?" Anson said, cutting into his chicken.

"Well, no. I guess we can't blame him for that. Some passing thug, but this other thing is something else besides." Davis chewed thoughtfully for a long moment, then went on, "I have a teenage daughter ... you never know; once a swine like that rapes a girl, he wants to rape another."

"Yeah," Anson said, but he wasn't interested. His mind went back to Meg. *Something has happened.* He only half listened to Davis as he talked on and on.

As Meg opened the front door, Anson said, "You're worrying me. I told you never to telephone me at the office."

"I had to see you," Meg said, leading the way into the sitting-room.

He took off his topcoat and joined her by the fire.

"What is it?"

"Sit down."

Impatiently, he sat on the settee and she sat on the floor at his feet.

"John ... this now isn't going to work. We're leaving here."

Anson stiffened. A cold void began to form inside him.

"*Leaving*? What do you mean?"

"Just that. Phil told me last night. We are going to Florida at the end of the month."

"Florida?" Anson stared at her. "Meg! What are you telling me?"

She gave a hopeless shrug.

"That's what he told me. Some man ... his name is Herman Schuman ... has a big horticultural set-up in Florida. He happened to be in Framley's stores a couple of days ago. He saw what Phil could do. He's offered him a partnership. Phil is wild with excitement. It's exactly what he wants and no risks."

Anson sagged back against the cushions of the settee. "At the end of this month?"

"Yes. Phil's giving in his notice at the end of the week. And there's something else. He intends to cancel the insurance policy. He doesn't need the capital now."

"You'll go with him?" Anson asked.

"What else can I do?" Meg suddenly gripped his hands. "Oh! John! I want you so much! What can we do?"

He pulled her to him. His mind tried to cope with what she had told him.

Florida! She would be miles away from him! The thought of losing all that money that he had counted on, had dreamed about, sent a stab of frustration through him.

Meg pulled away from him and got to her feet. She began to move restlessly around the room.

"You see now? I had to telephone you! Can't we get rid of him before he leaves? That's our only hope, John. If we can get rid of him before the end of the month ..."

"Yes ... let me think," Anson said, pressing his hands to his head. "How long have we ... eighteen days before the end of the month?"

"Yes."

Anson felt a sudden chill of apprehension.

"There's Maddox!"

"Oh damn Maddox!" Meg exclaimed. "If we don't do it before the end of the month, we'll never do it! John! I'm willing to take a risk ... are you?"

"But how?" Anson asked, wavering. "I imagined I had five months to get this fixed ... now I have only eighteen days!"

Meg drew in a quick, sharp breath. She had him hooked! For the past days and nights she had thought and thought how she could persuade him to kill her husband before she lost Sailor Hogan. It had come to her suddenly to tell Anson that Phil would be leaving the district at the end of the month. She knew she would be safe telling him this. He would never think to check.

Anson was now facing her.

"This is something I must think about," he said. "Meg, may I stay the night?"

94

With him on the hook, she could afford to be generous. After all, in the past she had slept with dozens of less savoury men than Anson.

"Of course ..."

She came to him and putting her arms around him, she pressed herself against him, trying to control the shudder of revulsion that went through her at the touch of his hands.

For the past hour, Anson had been lying on the bed, sleepless. The time was after three o'clock a.m. The white light of the moon fell across the bed, lighting the hollows and the curves of Meg's naked body as she lay sleeping by his side.

Suddenly Anson's mind became alert. For no reason at all, he thought of Harry Davis and the conversation they had had together over lunch. He remembered what Davis had said: *I have a teenage daughter ... you never know, once a swine like that rapes a girl, he wants to rape another.*

He sat up abruptly.

"Meg!"

Meg's quick, light breathing faltered. She stirred and became awake.

"Meg!" Anson gripped her arm. "Wake up! I want to talk to you!"

She moaned, then half sat up.

"What is it?"

"Have you yesterday's newspaper?"

She stared at him as if she thought he had gone crazy.

"Newspaper? Yes ... it's downstairs."

"Get it! Make some coffee! Come on, Meg, wake up! I have an idea ... get moving!"

Still dazed with sleep, but urged on by his tone, Meg slid out of bed and put on her wrap. She walked unsteadily to the door.

"Hurry!" Anson exclaimed.

He turned on the light and pulling the sheet over him, waited impatiently for her return.

After some minutes, she came back into the room, the newspaper under her arm, carrying a tray with the coffee things.

Anson snatched the newspaper from her and read the headlines as she poured two cups of coffee.

"What is it?" she asked.

When he waved her to silence, she shrugged and sat on the foot of the bed, sipping her coffee and watching him.

After some minutes, Anson let the paper drop and took the cup of coffee she handed to him.

"I think I've got it!" he said. "See this?" He pushed the newspaper towards her, pointing to the headlines.

Still dazed, Meg stared at the paper, then at Anson.

"I don't understand!"

Impatiently, Anson pointed to the headlines.

MANIAC KILLS YOUTH:
GIRL COMPANION ASSAULTED.

"A nut like that always strikes again," Anson said. "We're going to make use of him. He's going to kill Barlowe and attack you! Even Maddox will have to accept a situation like that!"

Meg stared at him as if she thought he had gone out of his mind.

"What are you saying ... *attack me*?"

Anson finished his coffee and set down the cup. "It says here the police are warning all courting couples that this man might strike again. This means the police *expect* him to strike again! Can't you see this is just the set-up we are looking for?" He threw the paper aside. "The girl has given the police a description of the man. She says he is short with a fat face and staring eyes. He was wearing a black topcoat and a black slouch hat. When she was struggling with him, his hat fell off: he was as bald as an egg. What a description! This is the man who is going to murder Barlowe! You will give the police his description! They are waiting for him to kill and rape again! They'll accept what you say without question! This is the foolproof way to get rid of your husband and get the money!"

Meg remained motionless, her mind slowly grasping what he was saying.

"Didn't you say your wedding anniversary was coming up towards the end of the month?" Anson asked. "When is it exactly?"

Bewildered, Meg said, "Next Friday ... what has that to do with it?"

"Four days' time! It's exactly right! It has everything to do with it! You must persuade Barlowe to take you out to dinner, then after dinner, you must persuade him to drive out to some lonely spot ... Jason's Glen would do fine. I'll be there ... waiting."

Meg's eyes opened wide.

"And then ...?"

Anson pointed to the paper.

"That happens again."

Meg flinched.

"You mean ... you'll shoot Phil?"

"That's what I mean ... and attack you. Look, Meg, you can't expect to pick up fifty thousand dollars for nothing. You'll have to be found in such a state the police, and more important, Maddox, will have no doubt you were attacked by this maniac. You'll give them a description of the man who attacked you ... they won't suspect you ... they can't suspect me ... it's the perfect set-up!"

"But John ..."

"Don't argue about it!" Anson said impatiently. "This is the foolproof way we can do it in the time we have left. I'm certain Maddox won't be suspicious but if I tried some other way to get rid of Barlowe, Maddox would be suspicious. The trick with this set-up is the police expecting it to happen again! We have four days in which to work this out. We'll ..."

"John!" Meg's voice rose a note. "You must listen to me! I see it's a good idea, but you haven't thought enough about it. Suppose it rains? Phil wouldn't go out to Jason's Glen if it was pouring with rain."

Anson, impressed, nodded.

"You're right. We must hope it doesn't rain, but if it does, then I'll have to do it here. Your story will be you heard someone prowling around the house: Barlowe went to see who it was: you heard a shot: then this maniac came in and attacked you. It's better if we do it up at Jason's Glen, but if we can't, then we'll do it here."

"But suppose this man is arrested before Friday night? Suppose we don't know he has been arrested?" Meg said. "I'd look a fool giving the police a description of a man who is already in jail, wouldn't I?"

Anson stared at her for a long moment, then he nodded. "You're using your head," he said. "I missed out on that one, and it's important. I have yet to work out the details.

This is just the outline of the plan. We can get over that snag. You will be in such a state of shock after you've been attacked, you won't be able to be questioned for two or three days. In the meantime I'll have found out if this man has been arrested or not. Because you are the wife of one of my clients, I can send flowers to you. If this man has been arrested, I'll send you carnations. If he is still at large, I'll send you roses. You won't say a word to the police until you get flowers from me."

"What happens if he is caught?"

"We'll think up a description of some other man. It often happens that after an attack like this some other maniac gets inspired and does the same thing, but if we can give a description of the original killer we're in a much safer position."

There was something obviously worrying Meg and Anson, staring at her, sharply asked her what it was.

"I don't understand what you mean ... I'll be in such a state of shock ... what does that mean?"

Anson picked up the newspaper and tossed it to her.

"The girl was chased through a wood, knocked down, beaten up and then raped. She was in a hell of a state! Read it ... see for yourself! That's what has got to happen to you! This won't be play acting, Meg! Maddox will want the doctor's report. He has got to be convinced. It's up to you ... you either are ready to take it or you don't do it."

Meg walked over to the window. She lifted aside the blind and looked out into the dark night. A feeling of cold, sick fear was growing inside her. She thought of Hogan. *I want that money by the end of the month or you and me are through!* The thought of never seeing Hogan again, never feeling his hard, muscular arms around her, never hearing him cursing as he made love to her was something Meg couldn't contemplate.

She dropped the blind, turned and forced a smile.

"Of course, John ... anything you say ... anything you want me to do ... I'll do it."

Anson relaxed back on the pillow.

"Fine," he said. "I'll come out here next Thursday. I'll have everything fixed by then. Friday, we'll do it. Are you sure you can get your husband to take you out on Friday?"

"He'll take me out," Meg said. "You don't have to worry about that."

Anson held out his hand.

"Come here. In five days we'll be worth fifty thousand dollars! Imagine! Fifty thousand dollars."

Reluctantly, Meg crossed the room and let him pull her down beside him on the bed.

Jud Jones, the fat, sprawling night guard of Anson's office block, waddled out of his tiny office as Anson came from the elevator.

"Evening, Mr Anson," Jones said cheerfully. "You intend to work late tonight?"

"I guess so," Anson said pausing, "but don't bother about me. I'm just going out for a bite to eat, but I'll be back. I'll be through by eleven. Don't think it's a burglar if you see my light on."

Jones' fat face split into a leering grin.

"I know your habits by now, Mr Anson. I won't disturb you ... you sure must be busy."

Anson had made it his business to keep friendly with Jones. There had been times when Anson had taken a girl up to his office because he had been so short of money he couldn't afford a hotel. Jones had turned a blind eye when there was a light on in Anson's office after midnight. At Christmas, Anson had somehow found the money to tip Jones liberally. Jones knew all about Anson's girls and envied him his sexual prowess.

"Busy? I guess I am," Anson said. "Jud ..." He took out his wallet and selected a five-dollar bill. "I hate that shirt you're wearing ... buy yourself another." His grin told Jones he was fooling, but he wasn't fooling about the five-dollar bill.

"Sure will, Mr Anson, and thanks."

Jones' thick fingers closed over the bill.

"You won on something good, Mr Anson?"

"Got onto a fifty to one beauty," Anson lied, then nodding, he went out into the street. The time was half past eight. He walked over to Luigi's restaurant. While he ate the set dinner, he went over in his mind the plan he had concocted. He was satisfied that it would work. Meg would be in the clear. Now he had to be sure that he himself would also be in the clear.

His meal finished, Anson returned to his office.

He knew Jones' routine. At ten o'clock, Jones began his patrol of the building. He rode up in the elevator to each floor, made his patrol along the corridors and then returned to his cubby hole of an office at eleven thirty. At one fifteen he made a second patrol.

Anson sat at his desk. He switched on his tape recorder, put on a new reel of tape and placed the microphone close to his typewriter. He fed paper into the typewriter then pressed down the start and record buttons on the recorder. He began to type meaningless words for the next hour, recording the busy clicking sounds of the typewriter keys.

A few minutes past ten o'clock, he heard the whine of the elevator and he listened to Jones' heavy tread going past his office door. Anson kept on typing. When he heard the elevator whine again, taking Jones to the next floor, he switched off the recorder, put the reel of tape into one of his desk drawers, turned off the light and after locking up his office, he went down to the street.

Fay Lawley sat alone in the bar of the Cha-Cha Club nursing a whisky and soda. She was disgruntled. She had been sitting alone now for the past hour and no man had as yet approached her. She wasn't pleased when she saw Beryl Horsey, wearing a mink stole and diamond earrings come in, look around, spot her and with a wave of her hand come over.

Beryl was Joe Duncan's girlfriend and she had known Fay longer than Fay cared to remember.

"Hello there ... all alone?" Beryl asked.

"Waiting for someone," Fay said shortly. "How's tricks? Have one with me?"

"Can't stop. I'm expecting Joe." Beryl looked at Fay, screwing up her large violet coloured eyes. "Don't see you around with Johnny Anson any more. You two fallen out or something?"

Fay grimaced. "Who wants to go around with a cheap punk like him?" she said shrugging. "Can't even afford these days to buy a girl a drink."

Beryl lifted her painted eyebrows.

"Hey! Hey! Who's been kidding you? He's come into money, darling. He paid Joe all his debts ... a thousand and something. He's in the money." She smiled. "Maybe he's found someone else. I've got to fly."

She flicked painted nails along her mink stole, smiled and was gone.

Fay sat sipping her drink, a sudden vicious expression on her over-painted, coarse face.

A thousand dollars! Where could Anson have raised that kind of money? He never did have any money!

Fay finished her drink and stood up.

He'd had his fun with her. Now, if he had money, she was suddenly determined to have some of it. If he thought he could brush her off that easy, he had another think coming.

She left the bar and started down the street towards the nearest taxi rank.

A fat, elderly man moved into her path.

"Hello, baby," he said and closed one eyelid. "I'm looking for a naughty girl. Have I *found* one?"

Fay hesitated, then she flashed on her hard, brilliant smile. There was time to fix that rat Anson: a bird in the hand, she thought as she said, "Hello sweetheart. You and I must have the same ideas."

Sailor Hogan woke with a start. The telephone bell was ringing. Cursing, he half sat up on his big double bed. By his side was a redheaded, over-developed teenager who Hogan had picked up at the afternoon dance at the Blue Slipper club. She too had come awake and was staring owlishly at Hogan as he snatched up the receiver.

"Yeah? Who is it?"

"Jerry ... it's Meg."

His battle-scarred face showed angry impatience.

"You woke me up ... what's the fire about?" he snarled.

"He's going to fix it," Meg said breathlessly. "I must see you, Jerry."

Hogan suddenly became fully awake.

"He's really got it fixed?" he asked, sitting bolt upright. "For when?"

"This is Friday. He'll be here with the final plan on Thursday night. I must see you before then."

"You'll see me," Hogan said. "I'll be along tomorrow," and he hung up.

The redhead said peevishly, "Who's she? Who are you seeing?"

Hogan flopped back on his pillow. Although he had plenty of stamina, he was surprised to find that this teenager had exhausted him.

"That was my mother," he said. "What's eating you? A guy has to see his mother once in a while, doesn't he?" He reached out and grabbed her.

"I didn't know you had a mother," she said, her fingers digging into the thick muscles of his back.

"That's a nice thing to say," Hogan said, grinning. "How do you think I got here without a mother?"

The girl suddenly cried out and her long-nailed fingers began to scar Hogan's back.

Patty Shaw came into Maddox's office. She paused in the doorway when she saw Maddox was glaring at a policy he was holding in his hands.

"If you're busy, I'll come back," she said. Maddox dropped the policy on his desk, made a grimace of disgust, then reached for a cigarette.

"What is it?"

"Here's the Barlowe report from the Tracing Agency," Patty said. "Do you want to look at it now?"

"Barlowe?" Maddox frowned, then his face cleared. "Yeah ... the gardener. Sure I want to look at it now. You looked at it?"

"It'll interest you," Patty said and laid the file on his desk. "Not the husband ... he's just the run of the mill, but the wife ... oh, la! la!"

Maddox picked up the file.

"What does that mean ... oh, la! la!?"

"You'll see," Patty said, and swished her way out of the room.

Maddox lit another cigarette, pushed back his chair and began to read the neatly typed dossier.

7

On Thursday morning, Anson called in at an electrical store in Lambsville and bought a time switch clock. He asked the salesman to show him how it worked.

"This is designed," the salesman explained, "to turn on any piece of electrical equipment at any required time. It also turns the equipment off at any required time. For example, if you want a radio programme that comes on at ten o'clock, you set the hand of the clock to ten and the radio will automatically come on at this time."

Anson said he wanted the clock to boil water for his morning coffee.

"It's the perfect thing," the salesman said, "I use one myself."

At lunchtime, Anson went to the Marlborough restaurant. As he entered the bar, he ran into Jeff Frisbee, a reporter on the *Pru Town Gazette*.

"Hi, John," Frisbee said. "Have one with me?"

Anson said he would have a Scotch. While they were waiting for the drinks to be set up, Anson asked Frisbee if he was lunching.

"I haven't the time," Frisbee said. "I have two murders in my hair and the old man expects me to write something about them every day. I'm running myself ragged trying to find something to write about."

"The Chief of Police doesn't seem to be getting anywhere," Anson said, saluting Frisbee with his glass before drinking. "This maniac ... still no trace of him?"

"No, but the Chief is a wily bird. He may not be giving any secrets away. He told me that he is convinced the heistman who killed Patrol Officer Sanquist was an out-of-towner, but he's convinced this maniac is a local man."

"What makes him think that?" Anson asked.

"He figures no one but a local man would know Glyn Hill. It's way off the beaten track. No passing motorist would ever find it."

"A man as bald as an egg shouldn't be so hard to find."

"That's a fact, but the Chief isn't a hundred per cent sure the girl was right when she said the guy was bald. She was in a hell of a panic. Could be he had white hair or very fair hair and he looked bald to her in the moonlight."

"Well, I guess it isn't too tough to check every blond or white headed man in the district and find out what he was doing at the time of the killing," Anson said.

Frisbee, whose hair was as black as a raven's wing, looked at Anson's blond hair and grinned.

"Just what were you doing at the time?"

Anson forced a laugh.

"In the sack with my local homework," he said and winked.

"Anyway, according to the girl, this guy was in his fifties and fat ... that's something you aren't," Frisbee said. "I guess she was lucky to come out of it alive."

When Frisbee had left, Anson went into the restaurant. So far then, he told himself, the maniac hadn't been found, but there were still lots of hours to get through before he killed Barlowe, and during those hours the maniac could be arrested.

After lunch, Anson continued his routine calls. Around seven thirty, he drove out to the Barlowe house, and put his car in the garage. He rang the front door bell and the door was immediately opened by Meg.

He followed her into the sitting-room. In the light of the shaded lamp, he saw she looked pale and there were dark smudges under her eyes. She looked as if she had been sleeping badly.

"What's wrong?" he asked, taking her in his arms. "You look tired. What's the matter?"

She pushed him away.

"Wrong? You ask what's the matter?" She faced him angrily. "This thing is on my mind! I can't sleep. How would you like to sleep in the same house with someone you are planning to murder? You ask what's wrong? Are you that insensitive?"

Anson lifted his shoulders.

"You made your mind up to go ahead," he said. "You should have no regrets."

She sat on the settee, her clenched fists resting on her knees.

"I can't believe it is going to happen tomorrow night!"

"It depends on you," Anson said, sitting beside her. "Can you get him out to Jason's Glen? The forecast is good ... it won't rain. If you can get him out there, then it's fixed."

Meg moved uneasily.

"Yes ... I'll get him out there," she said. "We are going to have dinner at the Court roadhouse. After, I'll make him take me to Jason's Glen."

"I was out there last night," Anson said. "There's a telephone call box on the highway about a half a mile from the glen. I'll be waiting there. I want you to call me and let me know for certain if you are coming. If something goes

108

wrong, and he insists on returning home, I must know." He took from his wallet a scrap of paper which he gave to her. "That's the number of the call box. I'll be waiting from ten o'clock onwards."

She nodded, putting the paper in her bag.

"When you get to the glen," Anson went on, "stay in the car, but keep the windows down."

Meg shuddered.

"I understand."

"When I've got rid of him," Anson said, staring into the fire, "I'll have to work on you." He reached out and put his hand over hers. At his touch she closed her eyes. "You're going to get hurt, Meg. We daren't take any chances. You'll have to be brave about this ... you understand? You mustn't blame me. What I do to you will convince Maddox and the police you are in the clear. The doctor must be convinced that this isn't a faked attack."

She felt a chill creep up her spine, but thinking of Sailor Hogan, she nodded.

"It's all right ... I understand."

"From the glen to the highway is about a quarter of a mile," Anson said. "You'll have to get down to the highway. He'll be in the driving seat. You won't be able to use the car. It may take some time before passing motorists see you. You must fake you're unconscious. Remember, you say nothing until you get flowers from me. If you get carnations, you'll know the maniac has been caught. If you get roses, you'll know he's still at large." He took a folded paper from his wallet. "Here is a description of a man I have made up. You'll use this if the maniac has been arrested. You understand all this?"

"Yes."

"That's about it," Anson said. " Don't let them rattle you and don't say a word until you see my flowers. The doctor won't let the police worry you until he is sure you are good and ready."

She looked at him, her eyes dark ringed and scared.

"You are sure this is going to work?" she asked. "You're sure we'll get the money?"

"We'll get it," Anson said. "With this set-up we can't go wrong. You'll have the public's sympathy and Maddox will know if he tries to block your claim, it'll be bad publicity and he hates that. I'll work on the reporters. Yes ... we'll get the money all right."

Meg, still thinking of Hogan, said, "I can't believe it's going to happen."

"In a couple of weeks, you'll be worth fifty thousand dollars!" Anson said. "We'll go away together! You, me and fifty thousand dollars!" He put his arm round her. "Together with that kind of money, we'll take the sun out of the sky!"

"Yes."

Meg broke away and went over to the fire.

Anson stood up.

"I mustn't forget the gun," he said and crossed to the sideboard and took the wooden box from the drawer. From it, he took the gun and six cartridges.

Watching him with growing horror, Meg said, "You'll have to leave now, John." She felt she couldn't bear to have this cold-blooded planner of murder any longer in the room. "Phil is coming back. He said he would be back by nine."

Anson turned and stared at her; a surge of angry disappointment ran through him.

"I thought we were going to spend the night together. Why is he coming back?"

"He has given up his classes now he is going to Florida," Meg lied. "He is seeing this man he's doing the deal with, then he's coming home. You really must go, John. He mustn't see you as you go down the lane."

A sudden cold suspicious expression came into Anson's eyes.

"You're not falling out of love with me, are you?"

"Of course not ... but you take all this so calmly. I'm frightened. I'll do it with you, but I can't be so, so cold-blooded about it as you are."

"This man is nothing," Anson said. "Fifty thousand dollars will mean everything to us. I'm not being cold-blooded ... it is a matter of how much you want the money."

"You must go ... look at the time."

"I'll be waiting for your telephone call," Anson said. "Remember what I've told you. It'll work." He picked up the gun and put it in his pocket. "Come here, Meg ..."

She forced herself to go to him. His kisses made her feel physically ill and the feel of his hands as they moved down her back made her cringe.

She pushed away.

"You must go!"

He looked at her for a long moment, then nodded and went out to his car.

She sank onto the settee, her hands to her face, shuddering.

Sailor Hogan came out of the kitchen where he had been listening to everything that had been said.

"Well, you nearly balled up everything," he said, coming into the room. "What's the matter with you? Why didn't

111

you love the guy a little? He was wanting it. Now you've sent him away with a bee in his workbox."

"I hate him!" Meg said. "He terrifies me."

"What's the matter with you? He's smart and he means business. He's quite a boy with his talk of taking the sun out of the sky ... I dig for that."

Meg jumped up and put her arms around Hogan's thick muscular shoulders.

"Love me, Jerry," she said, her lips lightly touching his thick coarse skin. "Please love me."

With a bored grimace, Hogan swung her down onto the settee.

At half past five on Friday evening, Anna Garvin pushed aside her typewriter, collected the papers on her desk and put them in one of her desk drawers.

"Time to go home, Mr Anson," she said as she got to her feet.

Anson regarded her as he leaned back in his desk chair. His desk was covered with papers which he had deliberately laid out to create an impression that he was busy.

"You run along, Anna," he said. "I've still a few things to clear up."

"Can't I help?"

"No ... I'm just killing time. This is nothing urgent. I just don't happen to be in a rush to get home."

When Anna had gone, Anson scooped up all the papers on his desk and pushed them into a file. He then took from his desk drawer the time switch clock he had bought the previous day. He read the instructions again, then plugged the gadget in to the mains socket. To the lead from it, he plugged in a two-way adapter to his tape recorder and his desk lamp.

He then set the switch to operate in five minutes and he sat back, lit a cigarette and waited. After five minutes had crawled by, his desk lamp suddenly came on and the tape recorder started up, playing back the tape he had made of his typing. He turned up the volume until he was satisfied the sound of the typing could be heard in the corridor. He waited another five minutes, then he watched the desk lamp go out and the recorder stop.

He then reset the time switch to come into operation at nine thirty. He set the turn off hand of the clock to eleven. Satisfied the gadget worked, he locked up his office and rode down in the elevator to the ground floor.

He found Jud Jones reading the evening newspaper in his office.

"Jud ... I'll be working late tonight. Don't think I have a burglar in my office."

Jones grinned and winked.

"That's okay, Mr Anson. I won't disturb you."

"This is work, Jud, so take that leer off your face," Anson said grinning. "I'm going out to supper, then I'll be back."

"Okay, Mr Anson, have you your key?"

"Yeah ... see you," Anson nodded and went out into the street.

He had a light supper and then drove to his apartment. He cleaned and loaded Barlowe's gun. Putting the gun in his topcoat pocket, he went down to his car.

The time was now eight o'clock. He drove back to his office. Parking his car some way from the entrance to the block, he entered the block. He walked to Jones' office.

"I'm back," he said, "I'll be working to around eleven."

Jones shook his head.

"You watch out, Mr Anson ... the way you work, you could get an ulcer."

"I'll watch it," Anson said, and he went over to the elevator and rode up to his floor. He waited a few moments, then silently walked down the stairs and left the office block. He got in his car and drove fast to the Brent–Pru Town highway.

When he was in sight of the telephone call box, he pulled off the highway onto a lay-by, turned off the car's lights and lit a cigarette. He had a long wait ahead of him.

He relaxed in the driving seat, aware of the weight of the gun in his pocket, his mind probing the plan he had made. He could find no flaw in it.

At twenty minutes to ten, he left the car and walked to the call box. He sat on the dry earth behind the box out of sight of the passing motorists and waited. Again he had a long wait. The minutes crawled by and he was beginning to wonder if something had gone wrong when the telephone bell in the call box began to ring. He opened the door to the call box and picked up the receiver.

Barlowe was startled when Meg had suggested they should go to the Court roadhouse to celebrate their wedding anniversary.

Meg had appeared while he was eating his breakfast. She had on her soiled green wrap and her hair was tousled. She leaned against the doorway, a cigarette between her full lips and Barlowe, looking at her, felt faint desire stir in him.

"We haven't been out for months," Meg said. "I'm sick of hanging around this dump. If you don't want to take me, say so, I'll go alone."

Barlowe said, "A place like that costs money ..."

114

"Well, spend some money for a change," Meg said. "I want to get drunk tonight." She stared at him. "There are other things I want to do tonight as well."

They looked at each other for a long moment, then she turned and went upstairs to her room.

Barlowe pushed aside his half-eaten breakfast and leaned back in his chair. Meg would have been surprised and shocked if she knew what was going on in his sick mind. He was no longer interested in her. That moment when he had laid hands on the screaming, terrified girl had been the most exciting and sensational thing that had happened to him in his life.

The living and the dead, he thought and got to his feet. The man rolling out of the car, shot through the head, and the girl struggling and screaming. Meg was poor stuff to such an experience, but if she wanted to be taken out, he'd better take her out. He was now nervous that anyone should suspect that he had done this thing. He had put the gun, the white bathing cap and the cheek pads under the floorboards in his room. He wanted to have the chance of doing this act of violence many times ... he had no intention of being caught.

Tomorrow night, he intended to go out again on the prowl. He would try Jason's Glen this time. He might be lucky to find two young people up there alone.

It startled him when they had finished a good, but expensive dinner and had returned to the bar for another drink that Meg should say she wanted to go out to Jason's Glen.

"What for?" Barlowe asked, slightly fuddled by the drinks he had taken. "I want to go to bed now." He stared at her, frowning. "I've had enough of this."

"Well, I haven't," Meg said. "What's the matter with you? Don't you want to be romantic?"

"With you?" Barlowe grimaced. "After all this time? What's come over you ... you're drunk!"

"All right, so I'm drunk," she said. "I'm sick of living like a nun. Even a drip like you is better than nothing the way I feel. Let's go!"

Barlowe shook his head.

"I'm not going, I'm going home." He thought of tomorrow night; the anticipation of the excitement and the violence made him break out into a sweat. "That place is for courting couples, not for people like you and me."

She leaned close to him. He could smell the gin on her breath. "You're coming with me. You'd better! If you don't, I'll go out there alone and find someone."

"I'm not going!" Barlowe said and became aware that the negro bartender was listening and staring. He lowered his voice. "I've had enough of this. I'm going home."

"Then I'll take the car and you can walk home," Meg said. "I'm going! You do what you like."

Barlowe hesitated. After all, he thought, it might be an idea to go out there. He hadn't been to Jason's Glen for months. By going out there now, he would get an idea of how many cars were there ... the lay of the ground.

"All right ... have it your way," he said, shrugging. "Then we'll go."

"I'll get my things," Meg said, and leaving him, she went into the ladies' room.

She paused, aware that her heart was hammering and she was breathing unsteadily. For a long moment she stood undecided, then with an effort, she went to the telephone booth and shut herself in.

Anson, the telephone receiver hard against his ear, said, "Yes?"

There was a pause, then he heard a woman's voice say, "Go ahead please," then Meg came on the line.

"Hello?" He recognised her voice. "Hello?"

"We are leaving now."

He realised how tense she was from the hysterical shrillness of her voice.

"It'll be all right," he said and hung up.

He returned to his car and drove up the narrow dirt road that led to Jason's Glen. He was a little uneasy. There was a remote chance some other couple might be in the glen. He arrived at the top of the steep road and then drove into the glen. There was plenty of room for cars to be parked and he drove his car between two overgrown shrubs and turned off the car's lights. He got out of the car and walked onto the open plateau that gave onto a wide and fine view of the lights of the town below.

Usually at this time of night, the plateau was crowded with cars, but this night it was deserted. Courting couples, neckers and smoochers were staying clear of such spots. The police warning that the sex killer might strike again had made an impression.

Anson looked around, then he selected a clump of shrubs that offered concealment. He pushed his way into them and sat down on the sandy, dry ground. He took out the gun and slid back the safety catch.

While he waited, he thought with satisfaction that the time switch clock in the office was creating a foolproof alibi for him. Light would now be showing through the frosted panel of his office door and when Jud Jones passed on his patrol, he would hear the busy clack of the typewriter from the tape recorder.

It would take Barlowe and Meg some thirty minutes to get from the roadhouse to the glen. Anson didn't expect them to arrive before ten thirty.

As he waited for them to arrive, he fingered the gun, his mind preparing himself for the moment when his finger would take up the slack of the trigger, when the gun would go off and when Barlowe would slump forward, a dead man.

Anson was again surprised by his own calmness and his feeling of complete indifference. He was now experiencing the same feeling that had come to him when he had shot the patrol officer. The death of the big, red-faced cop had meant nothing to him as the death of Barlowe would mean nothing to him when it happened.

A little after ten thirty, he heard the distant sound of an approaching car.

His fingers tightened on the butt of the gun. He half stood up, crouching in the shrubs as he listened. Then he saw the approaching lights of the car.

He watched the shabby Lincoln pull up within twenty feet or so from where he was concealed. Before the headlights went out, he saw the outlined heads of Meg and Barlowe.

In the silent stillness, he heard Barlowe say, "Well, here we are. There's no one here ..."

Anson moved silently out of his hiding place and started across the open space towards the car.

"Well, here we are," Barlowe repeated, his pale brown eyes roving around. He noted there were no cars except his own. A sudden, cold murderous thought dropped into his mind. Why not get rid of Meg? They were alone together. He could do what he liked with her in this loneliness. Then reason made him hesitate. Careful, he told himself. You can't do a thing like that ... they'd know you had killed her and they would then know you had done the other thing.

By now Anson had reached the car. He saw the driver's window was down. He could see Barlowe clearly in the moonlight.

Meg said, her voice unsteady, "Don't you want to make love to me?" Then suddenly, her nerve cracked, and she put her hands to her face. She screamed; "No! Don't do it, John ... don't do it!"

As Barlowe turned towards her in startled surprise, Anson lifted the gun and gently squeezed the trigger.

Meg was still screaming hysterically as the gun went off. Barlowe slumped forward; blood sprayed over the windshield.

Anson dropped the gun into his pocket, then he walked around the car and opened the off-side door. Meg threw up her hands to ward him off.

She was screaming hysterically as he dragged her out of the car.

PART TWO

8

Steve Harmas walked into the office, put his hat on the peg behind the door, then lowered his long frame into his desk chair.

He and his wife, Helen, had been to a party the previous night which had turned out to be a marathon drinking spree and Harmas was now suffering from a hangover.

He rubbed his forehead, grimaced, then looked with glazed eyes at the mail neatly laid out on his blotter.

There didn't seem to be anything that needed his immediate attention and he relaxed back and closed his eyes. He thought enviously of his wife still asleep.

The sudden sound of the intercom buzzer made him wince. He flicked down a key, said, " Harmas. Yeah?"

"I want you."

There was no mistaking Maddox's voice.

"I'm on my way," Harmas said, flicked up the key, pushed himself out of his chair and started the long tramp down the corridor to Maddox's office.

Patty greeted him with a bright smile that made Harmas wince.

"You're looking like a man with a hangover," she said. "Do you feel that way?"

"Yeah." Harmas held his head. "What's he want?"

"I don't know. I took the newspaper into him about five minutes ago. There was an explosion, then I heard him yelling for you."

"I have an idea that this isn't going to be my favourite day," Harmas said entering Maddox's office.

Maddox was smoking furiously. Although it was only a quarter after nine a.m., from the state of his desk and floor, he might have been working throughout the night.

"Look at this," he said and tossed the newspaper at Harmas.

Harmas sank into a chair and read the banner headlines.

MANIAC STRIKES AGAIN:
CARBON COPY MURDER AND ASSAULT.

He glanced at Maddox who was watching him, then he began to read the small type under the headline. Suddenly, he stiffened.

"Philip Barlowe? He's a client of ours, isn't he? Isn't he the one ...?"

"He *was* our client!" Maddox said, a snarl in his voice. "He was insured for fifty thousand dollars ... now he's dead!"

"Shot through the back of his head ... his wife raped!" Harmas looked shocked. "It's time they caught this nut. She sounds in a bad way."

"I can read," Maddox said, "Steve, I don't like this. There's a smell to it. This guy took out a life coverage ten days ago ... now he's dead. I don't like it."

"I guess she doesn't like it either," Harmas said a little impatiently. "It's one of those things." He looked sharply at

Maddox. "You don't think he was killed for the insurance money?"

"I don't know, but when a two-bit salesman insures his life for fifty thousand dollars and then he dies before the ink's scarcely dry on the policy, I don't like it."

"It says here she was raped and is suffering from a dislocated jaw. She gets the money, doesn't she? Don't tell me ..."

"For fifty thousand dollars I'd be raped and have my jaw dislocated," Maddox said grimly. "I'm a head start on you. You haven't seen the dossier the Tracing Agency turned in on this woman ... I have. It's some story. A woman like that could do anything."

"Where's the dossier? Let me see it, then I can look and act as clever as you," Harmas said.

"Never mind about the dossier. We've got to move fast. I want you to go to Brent right away. See Lieutenant Jenson. Tell him I don't like the set-up and that I want you to work with him. He'll be glad to have you. I want you to be there when Jenson talks to this woman. Keep your eyes and ears open. See Anson. Warn him I'm going to fight her claim when she puts it in. I don't want him shooting his mouth off to the press. Go to Jason's Glen or whatever it's called and look around." He stubbed out his cigarette and lit another. "And Steve, while she's in hospital, go out to her house and look around. Don't tell Jenson you're going."

"What am I supposed to be looking for?" Harmas asked.

"I don't know. Get the feel of the place. You might find something. Get out there and look."

"Well, okay," Harmas got to his feet. "I'll see Jenson first."

"Get the doctor's report about this woman. I want to be satisfied she was raped and attacked."

123

"It says so here, doesn't it?" Harmas pointed to the newspaper.

"Do you believe everything you read in papers?" Maddox snapped. "Get the doctor's report!"

A few minutes to nine o'clock, Anna Garvin arrived at the office. She was surprised to find Anson already at his desk.

"You're early," she said, then looked at her watch. "Or am I late?"

Anson had arrived some thirty minutes ago. He had come to the office early to disconnect the time switch clock and remove the tape on the recorder before Anna arrived.

"I'm early," he said. "Seen the paper? Barlowe's dead ... you remember ... the guy I sold that big policy to."

"Yes, I saw it. It's awful, isn't it, Mr Anson? I'm scared to go out at night."

Anson dialled the *Pru Town Gazette*. He asked to speak to Jeff Frisbee.

When the reporter came on the line, Anson said, "This guy Barlowe ... I sold him a fifty thousand dollar life coverage only a few days ago. I thought you might want that bit of news."

"Why, sure," Frisbee said. "Thanks a lot. Fifty thousand, huh? That's quite a hunk of dough. Well, his wife will welcome it. I'm glad you told me."

"There's been no arrest yet?" Anson asked.

"No. Jenson's going round like a zombie ... he hasn't a clue."

"How's Mrs Barlowe?"

"Pretty bad. The doctor won't let anyone talk to her."

"If you hear anything, let me know. I'm interested as Barlowe was my client."

"Sure will. How soon will your people pay the claim?"

"Shouldn't take long."

"Let me know when they do. It's news. I'll let you know anything of interest from my end."

Anson said he would and hung up.

"How is she?" Anna asked.

"Pretty bad. This is a horrible thing. I think the least I can do is to send her some flowers. Call up Devons and tell them to send a dozen roses right away to the hospital, will you, Anna?"

Lieutenant Fred Jenson of the Brent homicide squad was a chunky, fair man with alert grey eyes and a brisk manner. He wasn't much of a policeman, but he did try and sometimes, but not often, his efforts were rewarded.

He was flicking through a file when Harmas walked in.

"Hello," he said. "What do you want?"

He had worked with Harmas in the past and the two men got along well together. Harmas sat astride a straight-back chair.

"Maddox sent me down," he said. "Barlowe ... we have him covered for fifty thousand and Maddox is laying a square egg."

Jenson, who knew Maddox, grinned.

"Fifty thousand! I'll say the egg's square! So what? Don't tell me he's trying to make a mystery out of this one! It happened five days ago ... it's happened again. We have a sex killer in the district: it's as simple as that. Catching a punk like this isn't easy. I'm planning to plant a police officer and a girl out at Glyn Hill in the hope of trapping him."

"Maddox thinks this is a lot more complicated than that," Harmas said. "He's even thinking Mrs Barlowe shot her husband and raped herself to collect the fifty thousand."

Jenson moved impatiently.

"Maddox is crazy!" he exclaimed. "You don't mean this seriously, do you?"

Harmas shrugged.

"When can you talk to Mrs Barlowe?"

"Doctor Henry at the hospital said I could call him around six o'clock. He thought she might be ready to be interviewed by then."

"I'd like to come along. I won't be in the way. Maddox wants me to be around and help where I can. Fifty grand is lots of folding money."

"Okay. You help me ... I'll help you, but Maddox is just shooting at the moon."

"Yeah ... I've said time and time again that he's shooting at the moon, then what happens? The sonofabitch hits the moon!"

Jenson looked sharply at him.

"You don't really think Mrs Barlowe is involved in this killing?"

"I'll tell you after I have talked to her," Harmas said. "I'll be happier too, when I have talked to Doctor Henry."

"This is wasting time. This killer hit her so hard that he dislocated her jaw. Don't tell me ..."

Harmas lifted his shoulders.

"Maddox says for fifty thousand bucks, he would let anyone dislocate his jaw."

Jenson stubbed out his cigarette.

"Maddox! The fact is he doesn't want to meet Mrs Barlowe's claim! That's the long and short of it! He'd believe any story so long as he doesn't have to pay out and you know it."

126

"I guess you're right," Harmas said. "Well, I'll get along. I'll look in again around six o'clock. I want to be there when you talk to Mrs Barlowe."

Leaving police headquarters, Harmas drove over to Anson's office.

He had met Anson once before, but had only a vague recollection of him. He knew him to be a smart salesman but that was about all he did know about him.

He found Anson at his desk. As soon as he saw him, he remembered him: a man of middle height, blond, slimly built with grey, rather staring eyes.

"Remember me?" he said, offering his hand.

"Why, sure," Anson said. "It's Steve Harmas, isn't it?" He got up and shook hands. "Glad to see you. You've come about this shocking murder of Barlowe?"

Harmas was aware of the fat, homely looking girl at the other desk who was staring and listening.

"That's it," he said. "Look friend, I've just arrived from 'Frisco. How's about you and me going some place for a cup of coffee?"

"Why, sure," Anson said. "There's a place right across the road." To Anna he went on, "I'll be back in about an hour ... if anyone wants me."

A few minutes later, seated in a quiet corner in a café, Anson said, "Maddox on the warpath?"

Harmas grinned.

"That's an understatement. He thinks Mrs Barlowe shot her husband and raped herself!"

Anson dropped a lump of sugar into his coffee.

"The man's pathological. Well, he'll have to pass this claim! What's fifty thousand dollars to the National

127

Fidelity? The press know about it. If he tried to block payment, he's going to get some rank publicity."

Harmas stroked his nose. He looked thoughtfully at Anson.

"How come the press know about it? Did you tell them?"

"Why not?" Anson asked and sat back looking at Harmas, his grey eyes mildly enquiring. "Here we have a front page murder. Everyone in the district knows me. I sold Barlowe the policy. It's great publicity not only for me but also for the Company. It is this kind of publicity, providing the claim is paid, that sells policies."

"Maddox didn't want you to talk to the press," Harmas said.

"Why not?"

"He thinks the set-up stinks."

Anson smiled as he stirred the coffee.

"You work for him," he said. "I work for the Company. If I worked the way he wants a salesman to work, the Company would go broke. Come on ... you know that's right. Maddox should have retired years ago. He never gives a salesman a chance."

"When you turned in that policy," Harmas said, "Maddox didn't like it. He got a Tracing Agency to dig up some facts about Barlowe and his wife. He has a dossier on them both. I haven't seen it, but from what he tells me the wife hasn't anything to shout about. He told me a woman of her reputation could be capable of anything."

Anson suddenly slopped his coffee. He put down the cup and looked at Harmas, the grey of his eyes darkening.

"What's this dossier?"

"I don't know. I haven't seen it yet; that's what he says. He thinks she is capable of anything."

"He's crazy!" There was sudden doubt in Anson's voice. "This woman was attacked and raped! Hasn't he any feelings?"

"Jenson thinks the way you do," Harmas said quietly, "but I've worked with Maddox now for ten years. He has never been wrong when he claims a policy is off colour ..."

"This is a stunt to avoid meeting the claim," Anson said. "Maddox does more harm to the Company than you realise. What's fifty thousand dollars to a set-up like ours?"

"Fifty thousand dollars," Harmas returned and grinned. "Don't forget, Maddox gets two thousand or more claims a year. You work it out. One claim is nothing but two thousand claims add up to money."

Anson finished his coffee.

"Okay ... so what do you want me to do?"

"You don't do a thing. I just wanted to put you in the picture. I'm the guy who has to do the work. Where is Barlowe's house?"

Anson stiffened, then forced himself to relax, and as he lit a cigarette, he looked directly at Harmas.

"It's some way out of town and tricky to find."

"You take me there," Harmas said, getting to his feet. "I want to look it over."

"Look it over?" Anson said, not moving and staring up at Harmas. "What do you mean?"

"Maddox again. He wants me to look over the place while Mrs Barlowe is out of the way."

"But you can't do that! You can't break into ..."

"Come on!" There was a snap now in Harmas' voice. "I do what my boss tells me to do. Let's go."

Anson hesitated, then got to his feet. He followed Harmas across the street to where Anson's car was parked.

Harmas exclaimed, "Well! Look at this!"

He was staring at Barlowe's garden as Anson drove his car onto the tarmac of the drive.

"Pretty good, isn't it?" Anson said in a flat, cold voice.

"Good? Why, this guy must have been a genius! Look at those roses! Heck! I wish Helen could see them! She's always trying to grow roses!"

Harmas got out of the car and wandered around the garden. He stared at the goldfish; he gaped at the enormous dahlias; he admired the fountain while Anson stood by the car, watching him.

"Never seen anything to touch this," Harmas said eventually and turned to look at the house. "And take a look at this! What a contrast! Doesn't look as if he cared two hoots for his home, does he?"

Anson didn't say anything.

Harmas, his hands thrust deep into his trouser pockets, wandered with a long-legged stride up to the front door. He surveyed the peeling paintwork. He pressed against the door, then took something from his pocket and in a moment or so, the front door swung open.

"You can't go in there!" Anson said sharply. "Look Harmas ..."

But Harmas had already wandered into the hall and was now standing in the sitting-room.

Anson followed him in and watched him as he looked around.

"This is interesting," Harmas said. "A garden like that and yet these two were able to live this way. Look at this room! She couldn't have touched it in weeks. Look at the dust! What kind of a slut can she be?"

Anson said nothing. He watched Harmas wander over to the table and look at the portable typewriter and the mass of papers lying on the table.

"So she does some writing?" Harmas went on. "Or did he do it?"

"I don't know," Anson said, watching Harmas as he leaned forward and began to read some of the badly typed pages lying on the table. "Look, I don't think we should pry into these people's private papers."

Harmas suddenly pulled up a chair and sat down. For the next five minutes he turned the pages of the scattered manuscript, reading, a set, interested expression on his face.

Anson said curtly, "We have no right to be here. How much longer ...?"

Harmas raised his hand.

"Relax, friend. I'm investigating. Go sit in the car. Go look at the garden ... this is very, very interesting." He went on reading while Anson watched him. Finally, Harmas gathered together a number of pages he had been reading and folding them, put them in his pocket.

"What do you think you're doing?" Anson asked.

Harmas winked.

"You know, Maddox is something very special. He told me to come out here and look around. He had no idea what I was to look for and nor did I, but he told me to get the feel of the place." He tapped his pocket. "Believe it, or not, here is an outline for a short story of a woman who swindles an insurance company. She and her lover ... he is a ticket officer of an airline company ... it's a nice idea. Maddox will love it. If she wrote it, it shows she has had the idea of swindling an insurance company and when she puts in the claim, we can use this story to show the state of mind she's in."

"Look this is ridiculous," Anson said angrily. "Plenty of people write stories about ..." He stopped as he saw Harmas wasn't listening. Harmas had got to his feet and was now wandering around the room, whistling under his breath. He paused and peered at something hanging on the wall. "Well, seen this?" he said. "Barlowe was a pistol shot champion. He won first prize at the Pru Town Small Arms and Target Club."

"So what?" Anson said, an edge to his voice. "We'd look a couple of jerks if someone found us here."

"Relax," Harmas said. "Who's likely to come? Now a guy who is interested in pistol target shooting is likely to have a gun. I wonder if he did own a gun?"

"What does it matter if he did?" Anson said.

Harmas began moving around the room. He paused to open cupboards and drawers and finally he came to the ugly heavy sideboard. He pulled open a drawer.

"Here we are ... a gun box." He took the wooden box from the drawer and opened it. For a long moment there was a heavy silence, then he said "Cartridges, cleaning material, but no gun, and yet here's a place for the gun. Where's the gun?"

"Are you asking me or are you talking to yourself?" Anson demanded.

Harmas grinned at him.

"I was talking to myself. Look, why not go and admire the garden. I'm going to be here quite some time. This place fascinates me."

Anson went over to the settee and sat down.

"I'll stay here. If there is anything I can do ..." Harmas, humming under his breath, wasn't listening. He walked from the room and Anson listened to him climb the stairs.

9

An hour and a half later, Harmas and Anson drove away from Barlowe's house and towards Pru Town.

Harmas was silent for some time during the drive, then as they approached the outskirts of Pru Town, he began to talk.

"Maddox may seem to you to be a deadbeat always looking for trouble," he said, "but he's far from that. He's practically clairvoyant, and I'm not kidding. Here we have a situation: a man working as a small-time clerk, insures himself for fifty thousand dollars. Maddox was right to raise his eyebrows. Now I've seen this guy's home, I also ask myself why he should have insured himself for such a sum."

Anson hunched his shoulders.

"He wanted the policy to raise capital so he could start up on his own as a horticulturist," he said tonelessly. "I've already explained all this to Maddox. I didn't persuade Barlowe one way or the other if that worries you at all."

"He must have been planning something big," Harmas said, noting the irritation in Anson's voice. "Fifty grand is a hunk of dough for a little man like Barlowe."

"You've seen his garden," Anson said. "Why shouldn't he have big ideas? He was able to pay the first premium, so why should I worry?"

"He paid in cash?"

"Yes."

"From the look of the house, you wouldn't have thought he had that much money in cash."

Anson shrugged impatiently.

"Okay ... go ahead: make a mystery of it. He had the money: he gave it to me: do I have to get worried about a man giving me cash?"

Harmas glanced thoughtfully at the small, blond man at his side and then looked away.

"You're right," he said soothingly. "Tell me about Mrs Barlowe. What kind of woman is she?"

"I don't know," Anson said curtly. "I only saw her once ... she's good-looking, youngish. I didn't pay her much attention."

"Did they get along together?"

"Yes, they did," Anson said. "They got along very well together."

"Is that a fact? What makes you say that?"

Anson suddenly stiffened. Careful, he told himself, this guy isn't flapping with his mouth for the sake of making noises. He is the top investigator and Maddox's stooge.

"I don't know ... an impression I got. The way Barlowe spoke about her."

"He must have been smart to fool you," Harmas said, putting a cigarette between his lips. "You been upstairs and looked the set-up over?"

Anson's hands tightened on the steering wheel.

"Fool me? What do you mean?"

"They didn't sleep together. You should have seen his room. The sheets hadn't been changed in months." Harmas grimaced. "Our little pal was a pervert. I found some books in his room that would make your hair stand on end. There were other things too. Those two didn't live as husband and wife. I'm ready to bet a hundred bucks."

"Well, that's as it may be," Anson said tonelessly. "I had the impression that they were happy together."

"She kept the house like a pig sty. If a woman really loves her husband, she makes an effort to keep his home decent."

"That your idea?" Anson said indifferently. "It doesn't mean that to me. It just means she doesn't know how to run a house ... some women just can't."

"Well, we'll see. I just can't wait to read her dossier," Harmas said, lighting his cigarette.

"Just what is this dossier?" Anson asked, his voice sharpening.

"I haven't seen it yet, but Maddox is worked up about it."

"I'd like to see it," Anson said.

"You don't have to worry your head about all this. It's your job to sell insurance and you do it damn well. It's my job to make sure the policy is okay."

Some five minutes later, Anson pulled up outside the Marlborough hotel.

"I'll leave you here," he said. "I have still a lot of work to do."

"Fine," Harmas said, getting out of the car. "I have to see Jenson at six. We're calling on Mrs Barlowe. I'll let you know how it goes."

"Yes," Anson said, and waving his hand, he drove away.

Fay Lawley watched Harmas get out of Anson's car and walk over to the Marlborough hotel. She watched Anson drive away. She waited a moment, then crossing the street, she entered the hotel in time to see Harmas pick up his key from the desk and cross the lobby to the elevator.

She walked over to the desk where Tom Nodley, the clerk in charge, was busy sorting mail.

"Hi, Tom," she said and gave him her wide professional smile.

"Hello, baby," Nodley said, letting his eyes run over her lush body. "What do you want?"

"Who is the handsome Romeo who just picked up his key?" she asked, taking a dollar bill from her bag.

Nodley eyed the bill and grinned.

"He's no good to you, baby," he said and accepted the bill. "He's Steve Harmas: chief investigator National Fidelity Insurance."

Fay lifted her plucked eyebrows.

"Chief Investigator? Does that mean he is a cop?"

"Along those lines. He's checking on the Barlowe murder."

"But he is a cop?"

"You could call him that."

Fay smiled.

"Thanks ... be seeing you."

Nodley watched her ducktail walk to the exit with an appreciative stare.

Dr Henry, the house surgeon of the Pru Town hospital received Lieutenant Jenson and Harmas in his office. He waved them to chairs.

"This is Mr Harmas of the National Fidelity Insurance Corporation," Jenson explained. "Barlowe was insured by his company. He ..."

"Just a moment," Harmas broke in. He didn't want the doctor to get a wrong impression. "I'm an investigator and I'm working with the Lieutenant. My job is to check all claims made on our company. So far no claim has been made regarding Barlowe. There hasn't been time, but we want to be prepared when it is made. Barlowe was covered for fifty thousand dollars. He took out the policy about ten days ago. The circumstances are exceptional, but naturally, with such a sum involved, we don't want to pay it out if there is any doubt about the genuineness of the claim."

Dr Henry, a tall, balding man, lifted pale eyebrows. "What exactly do you mean by that and what has it to do with me?"

"We will need to be convinced that Mrs Barlowe was really attacked and raped," Harmas said. "We will need a certificate and details from you."

"I'll be happy to give you a certificate," Henry said. "The woman was most certainly attacked ... her jaw was dislocated, and there is no doubt she was brutally raped. I can give you details that must satisfy your people that she has been through a horrible and harrowing experience."

Harmas and Jenson exchanged glances. Harmas shrugged.

"Thanks, doctor, that's all we'll need. Can we talk to her now?"

"Yes. I'll take you to her." Henry looked at Jenson. "Make it as short as you can. She really is in a bad way, and she is still suffering from severe shock."

"Sure." Jenson got to his feet. "All I want at this stage is a description of the attacker. The rest of it can come later."

The two men followed the doctor up to the first floor. They entered a room in which was a bed and the usual hospital equipment. In the bed was a woman with auburn hair.

Motioning them to stay where they were, Henry went over to the woman.

"Mrs Barlowe, Lieutenant Jenson would like to talk to you. I've asked him not to bother you too much. Do you feel you can talk to him?"

While he was speaking, both Harmas and Jenson were looking curiously at the woman. Harmas was shocked to see that the left side of her face was heavily bruised and her left eye was half closed and swelling. There was split skin near her mouth. It was obvious she had taken a violent blow on the side of her face ... there was no fake about that. In spite of this disfigurement, Harmas saw that this woman was sensationally handsome ... beautiful, he decided, wasn't the right word.

"I'm all right," she said in a shaky whisper. "Yes, of course I'll talk to him."

Jenson came forward.

"You're not all right, Mrs Barlowe," he said. "I'm sorry to have to bother you at this time, but I want a description of the man that attacked you. Can you help me?"

Meg closed her eyes for a long moment, then opened them. On the table by the window was a vase holding a dozen blood-red roses.

If you get roses, you will know our man hasn't been arrested, Anson had said.

"He was short and thickset," she said, "and he was completely bald."

"That's the punk!" Jenson exclaimed, looking at Harmas. "The same one who ..." He paused, controlling his excitement. To Meg, he went on, "How do you know he was bald, Mrs Barlowe?"

She closed her eyes. There was a pause, then she said "In the struggle ... his hat fell off ... he had no hair at all."

"Can you remember what he was wearing?"

"A black coat and a black slouch hat."

Jenson nodded, satisfied.

"Okay, Mrs Barlowe, you take it easy. I won't worry you again for a while. You just relax."

Moving forward, Harmas asked, "Mrs Barlowe, there's just one thing that could help us. Why did you and your husband go out to Jason's Glen?"

The cobalt-blue eyes suddenly snapped open. Meg looked intently at Harmas.

"Why? Why ... Phil wanted to ... it was our wedding anniversary. He took me to the Court roadhouse ... he was in a romantic mood ..." She broke off and hid her face in her hands.

Dr Henry said, "That'll do for now, gentlemen. I want Mrs Barlowe to rest."

He shepherded Jenson and Harmas to the door. Harmas paused at the door and looked back at Meg. She lay motionless, her hands hiding her face.

As they walked down the corridor, Jenson said, "It's the same guy. The hell of it is he could be anywhere, and he could do this again."

"Let's take a look at Mr Philip Barlowe," Harmas said. "At least we won't be disturbing him."

"What do you want to look at him for?"

"I want to look at the man who managed to persuade that lush dish to marry him ... he should be quite a guy," Harmas said.

The morgue attendant, a burly negro, flicked back the sheet.

"Here he is mister ... ain't much to look at." Jenson, who had seen the body before, remained where he was, away from the table, his hand cupping a cigarette, his face showing impatience and irritation.

Harmas, his hat at the back of his head, surveyed what remained of Philip Barlowe. He stared for a long moment, then he nodded to the negro and turned to Jenson.

"Got a report on the slug that killed him?" Jenson squinted at him.

"Not yet ... why?"

"How long will it be?"

"Could be ready now."

"I have a hunch," Harmas said. "Let's find out if it is ready."

They walked to the Coroner's office and Jenson put a call through to the Ballistics department. While he was waiting, Harmas said thoughtfully, "What magic did a little punk like Barlowe have to persuade a sexy piece like that woman to marry him?"

"Women do odd things," Jenson said, then as the connection came through he waved Harmas to silence. He asked for the report on the bullet. There was a pause, then some talk, then Jenson said, "Okay, Ted. Thanks. I'll be right over," and he hung up. He stared at Harmas, his eyes puzzled. "Now what do you know? The two men were both shot with .38s, but the guns are different. The slugs don't match. How did you know?"

"I didn't," Harmas said. "I told you ... it was a hunch." He stood up. "It needn't mean a thing. Our bald-headed pal could own two .38 automatics ... but somehow I don't think he does."

A little after six o'clock, Anson completed his list of calls and then drove back to the Marlborough hotel. Right at this moment, he was thinking as he locked the car, Jenson and Harmas were seeing Meg. He would have given a lot to have been there. He had to trust her to keep her nerve. He wished he could call her later and find out what had been said, but that was far too dangerous.

This dossier, Harmas had spoken about ... what could be in it? Had Meg lied to him when she said she hadn't a record: nothing to hide? Had Maddox found out that she had had lovers? The more Anson thought about Meg, the more sure he was she couldn't have lived with Barlowe without having a lover. He had made a slip telling Harmas Meg and Barlowe had been happy together. He had forgotten they had had separate rooms.

"Hello, Johnny ..."

Anson started and looked round.

Fay Lawley stood by his side. She smiled at him, her eyes hard and glittering.

"Hello," Anson said curtly. He wasn't in the mood to be bothered with this overblown tart. "Excuse me. I have a business date ... I'm late already."

She caught hold of his arm.

"Skip it. Don't give me that line. I'm expecting you to take me out tonight and to spend some of your new-found money on me. It's time you unbuttoned your wallet."

Anson shook her hand off his arm.

"Beat it!" he said viciously. "Go, peddle it elsewhere," and pushing past her, he crossed the street and entered the hotel.

Fay stood motionless watching him disappear into the hotel, then with a hard little smile on her over-painted mouth, she started down the sidewalk to the nearest bar.

Maddox shoved aside a pile of papers that fell on to the floor. He lit another cigarette, ran his fingers through his hair and picked up yet another insurance policy from his in-tray.

Patty Shaw looked in.

"Steve's here," she announced.

141

Maddox said nothing for several seconds, then he put the policy down and stared at Patty. For some moments he didn't seem to register her, then his eyes became alert.

"Steve? Sure ... shoot him in."

Patty said to Harmas, "The Maestro is coming out of his trance. He'll see you."

Harmas entered the office and sat down in the client's chair. The time was nine fifteen a.m. He had driven through the night back to San Francisco and he was feeling jaded.

Maddox pushed back his chair.

"What's cooking?"

"Plenty," Harmas said, "but I haven't had the time yet to get it all straightened out. I thought I'd better come back here and talk it over with you. For a start: Barlowe and his wife didn't live as man and wife. They had separate rooms. He was a queer: a sick man. You should have seen the muck I found in his room: sadist stuff ... really rotten. Mrs Barlowe was attacked and raped. I have the doctor's certificate. Here are all the sordid details." He dropped a paper on the desk. "There's no fake about that. I've seen her. She's certainly been beaten up. I went over the house. She keeps it the way a self-respecting pig would hate. I've seen Barlowe. He's a shrimp of a man ... I can't think why she ever married him."

Maddox relaxed back in his chair. His red rubbery face creased into a benign grin.

"Go on ... keep talking."

"She writes short stories. Awful stuff, but one of them deals with an insurance swindle." Harmas took more papers from his pocket and dropped them on the desk. "Have a look at this when you have time. She has an idea."

Maddox nodded.

"Barlowe was a champion revolver shot," Harmas continued. "He owned a gun: a .38, but the gun is missing. Barlowe was shot with a .38. The other guy was also shot with a .38, but the slugs don't match. Mrs Barlowe gave out a description of the killer: a word for word description that appeared in the newspapers of the guy who attacked the other couple."

Maddox was practically purring. He opened his desk drawer, took out a file and pushed it towards Harmas.

"There it is, Steve. Take it away and read it. Then come back and we'll talk again ... you are doing fine."

Harmas picked up the file.

"There's one other thing," he said, getting to his feet. "Anson has already alerted the press that this woman is going to make a claim. If we block the claim without good reason, we're in for a lot of rank publicity. She has the sympathy of the public."

Maddox grinned wolfishly.

"You read that dossier. We can't get bad publicity once that dossier becomes public reading. This is a phoney claim. I knew it was as soon as it came to my desk. You keep going ... you're doing fine!"

Joe Duncan, a large man with a great sagging belly and a whisky complexion put down one of his six telephone receivers and looked questioningly at Sailor Hogan as he came into the office.

"Park your butt," Duncan said. "Have you any idea what the date is?"

Hogan settled himself in the big armchair opposite Duncan's desk. He struck a match to light a cigarette.

"Why should I care?"

"In five days you come across with twenty-five grand or you and me part company," Duncan said. He leaned his gross body back into his chair, reached thick fingers for a cigar, nipped off the end with his small yellow teeth and spat the end into the trash basket. "How's it coming? I want the dough ..."

Hogan grinned at him.

"You'll get it, even if I have to borrow it."

Duncan sneered.

"Who's going to lend you money?"

"You'd be surprised," Hogan said and winked. He was feeling very confident. "I'm a guy with prospects now."

Duncan tapped a copy of the *Pru Town Gazette* lying on his desk.

"From this rag, your meal ticket has been raped. Are you telling me you can still find twenty-five grand?"

Hogan's grin widened.

"Read it again. Who cares if she was raped? Her husband is dead and he was insured for fifty grand. Now put that in your gizzard and chew it over." He lounged to his feet. "Be seeing you, Joe. Relax. It's working out fine for me ... just relax."

When he had gone, Duncan scratched the back of his thick neck, shrugged and reached for the telephone.

10

Harmas arrived back in Pru Town late the following evening. He had spent all the morning with Maddox, and now briefed, was ready for action.

He dumped his bag at the hotel, then drove out to the Court roadhouse.

The roadhouse was situated a few miles outside Pru Town. It was one of those showy, neon-covered places that attracted the car trade and the young in search of a reasonably good dinner with a reasonably good band at a not too exorbitant price.

He walked into the bar, which, at that time, was nearly empty. He asked the barman, a big, jolly looking negro, if he could have a table in the restaurant. The negro said he would fix it. In the meantime, how's about a drink?

Harmas said he would have a large Scotch on the rocks and he sat at one of the high stools at the bar. He asked for the evening newspaper.

The negro got him the drink and the paper and then went to the far end of the bar to phone the restaurant. The front page of the *Pru Town Gazette* was given up to the Barlowe murder.

The barman came back to say a table would be ready in ten minutes.

"That's a horrible thing," he went on, seeing Harmas was reading about the murder. "These two were out here a couple of hours before it happened."

Harmas put down the newspaper.

"Is that right? It surprises me they went out to Jason's Glen. After the first murder you would have thought they would have kept clear of such a lonely place."

The barman rolled his eyes.

"That's just what he said. He didn't want to go. They argued about it for nearly twenty minutes, but she wanted it. Man! When a dame like that wants something, she gets it!"

"So he didn't want to go out there?"

"That's a fact. They came in here for a final drink. It was around half past nine. At one time I thought they would blow up, they got so heated. Finally, he said the hell with it: if she wanted to go that bad, then he would take her. Then she went to the Ladies' Room and kept him waiting for more than ten minutes. I saw he didn't go for that either!"

"Too bad she didn't take his advice," Harmas said, his mind busy. He finished his drink. "I guess I'll go and eat," and tipping the barman generously, he went in towards the restaurant.

He crossed the lobby and paused outside the ladies' room. The doorman glanced at him, then stiffened to attention as Harmas beckoned to him.

"Would there be a telephone in there?" Harmas asked and took out his wallet. From it he selected a five-dollar bill.

The doorman eyed the bill the way a gun dog eyes a falling grouse.

"Yes, sir."

"Automatic or does it go through a switchboard?"

146

"A switchboard, sir."

"I'd like to talk to the operator," Harmas said. He took out his card and let the doorman examine it. Then as he took the card back, he handed over the five-dollar bill.

"I can fix that," the doorman said. "Come this way." He took Harmas to a small office where there was a switchboard and a blonde thumping a typewriter. The blonde was young and pretty and she looked at Harmas as the doorman said, "This gentleman wants a little help." He winked. "You help him ... he'll help you." To Harmas, he said, "You go right ahead, sir. You'll find May ready to help helpful gentlemen," and he went away.

Harmas sat on the edge of the desk.

"Is that right, beautiful?" he asked and took out his wallet. He felt this was the right time to be extravagant. He knew Maddox would willingly meet any expense to save the company paying a phoney claim.

The blonde, snugly curved, with big baby-blue eyes, looked with alert interest as Harmas fished out a five-dollar bill.

"For that, handsome," she said, "you could go a very long way."

"That's good news," Harmas said, grinning, "but right now all I want is a little information. Do you keep a record of the outgoing calls you handle?"

"Yep." She looked him over. "Are you a private eye?"

"I'm private," Harmas said. "I'm trying to trace a call made from here on September 30th around half past nine ... made by a woman."

The blonde got to her feet and swung her neat hips over to the switchboard. She consulted a notebook.

"Here we are ... must be the one. I can't remember if it was made by a woman, but on that night I wasn't busy. I had only four calls. Three of them between seven and half past eight ... the other was around nine forty. Elmwood 68009."

"Could I have the other numbers?"

She gave him the numbers and he wrote them down, then he thanked her and passed over the five-dollar bill.

She smiled happily as she tucked the bill away. She was pretty, pert and sexy and for a brief moment Harmas regretted he was married, then he waved away such thoughts and went into the restaurant.

Later, he called police headquarters. The desk sergeant told him Lieutenant Jenson was still out.

"You could help me," Harmas said and introduced himself. "I want to know who operates on Elmwood 68009."

The Desk sergeant told him to hold on. After a delay he came back on the line.

"That's a public call booth on highway 57. If you have a Survey map of the district, the call box is in zone A.3."

Harmas thanked him, and hung up.

Around ten o'clock the same evening, Harmas walked down the long corridor that led to Jenson's office through the usual smell of disinfectant and sweat of a cop house.

Jenson, looking dirty and tired, was talking to someone on the telephone. When he saw Harmas, he said, "Well, keep after it ... yeah ... yeah ... call me back," and he hung up. He frowned at Harmas who was now sitting astride one of the hard-backed chairs. "What do you want?"

"I'm just back from seeing Maddox. He sends his love. How are you making out?"

Jenson rubbed the back of his neck. He looked like a man who had been under pressure for more hours than he likes to remember.

"One of my men was shot to death by a hold-up thug who cleaned out the Caltex cash box on the Brent highway a few days back. The same gun that shot my man, killed Barlowe."

Harmas drew in a long, slow breath.

"So what now?"

"We're checking on every bald-headed man in the district. We're hunting for the gun," Jenson said, his expression grim. "I have every man I can spare on the job."

"How much did the hold-up thug get away with?"

"A little over three thousand."

"Did you get a description of the guy?"

"Yeah ... not the same guy who shot Barlowe. This one was tall," Jenson leaned back into his chair, took a cigar from his desk drawer and lit it. "Here's something odd. We had a report from the Marlborough hotel that a hat and coat were stolen on the night of the robbery. The hat was Swiss style with a cord and feather ... the gunman had the same kind of hat. Could mean something. I had an idea that the gunman was passing through, but now I am beginning to wonder if he wasn't a local man."

"Who gave you a description of this guy?"

"The gas attendant."

"Could be he was in such a panic he has the description wrong. Could be the gunman is our sex killer."

Jenson blew smoke to the ceiling.

"I guess."

Harmas brooded for a long moment, then said, "I'd appreciate it if you'd take me out to Jason's Glen tomorrow

149

morning. I have an idea ... I could be wasting your time, but I don't think I am."

Jenson wiped his sweating face.

"I want to go out there myself. Okay, I'll pick you up. What's your idea?"

Harmas got to his feet.

"It'll keep ... then see you tomorrow," and he made for the door.

As Jenson was about to pull into the lay-by at the bottom of the dirt road leading to Jason's Glen, Harmas said sharply, "Hold it!"

Jenson trod on the brake and brought his car to a standstill.

"Before you muck up the ground," Harmas said, "let's take a look."

He and Jenson went over to the lay-by. On a patch of soft ground they came upon a deep impression of a tyre track.

Harmas stared at it.

"This could be too good to be true," he said. "If we find the same track at Jason's Glen, I'd say my hunch is paying off. Take a look at this ... see how the tyre is worn on the left side. It is as good as a fingerprint. If you saw it again would you recognise it?"

Jenson examined the track for a long moment, then he nodded.

"Yeah ... so what?"

"We'll go up to the glen and see if we can find the same impression there."

Jenson shrugged and returned to the car. With Harmas at his side, he drove up the narrow road that led to the glen.

It took the two men more than an hour of patient searching before Jenson came across the tyre track.

"Here it is," he called to Harmas who was on the far side of the glen.

Harmas joined him. The track was clear in the sandy soil. The two men squatted beside it.

"That's it!" Harmas' expression showed his excitement. "Who says I'm not one hell of a detective!" He moved back. "This guy drove his car between these two shrubs. The car would be out of sight ... yeah, that's it!"

"Will you quit talking to yourself and make with some explanations?" Jenson said. "You think this could be the killer's car?"

As they walked back to the car, Harmas said, "That's my bet. Remember I asked Mrs Barlowe why she and her husband came out here and she said he was in a romantic mood and wanted to?"

"Yeah ... go on."

"She let drop that they had gone to the Court roadhouse. I went out there last night and got talking to the barman. He says Barlowe didn't want to come out here and they almost had a stand-up fight before Barlowe finally agreed to bring her here. She went to the ladies' room and kept him waiting some minutes. I wondered if she had used the telephone. There's a record of all outgoing calls, and at the time she was in the ladies' room, there's a record of a call to Elmwood 68009. I checked and it's the number of the call box we've just looked at. I think Maddox is right as usual." Harmas shrugged. "He's always right. I think she and a boyfriend murdered Barlowe. The boyfriend was waiting for her to call, alerting him they were on their way. He then drove up there, hid his car and when they arrived, he shot Barlowe."

Jenson looked worried.

151

"Are you suggesting the boyfriend then attacked and raped her? To hell with that for an idea!"

"I'll quote Maddox. He said he would be happy to be attacked and raped for fifty grand."

"That's what Maddox says. A woman wouldn't ..."

"But we are one jump ahead of you," Harmas said. "We've turned a Tracing Agency onto this woman and they've come up with quite a dossier. She has not only been in jail for stealing, she was also a prostitute before she married Barlowe. I think Maddox is right. A woman like that wouldn't flinch from rough treatment if it gave her an alibi and earned her fifty thousand dollars."

"You think this sex killer is her boyfriend?"

"No. I think her boyfriend did the Caltex job, and he duplicated the sex killing as a front. The fact your patrol officer and Barlowe were killed by the same gun, points to it."

"If these two were going to horn in on a fifty thousand dollar insurance," Jenson said, "why should he risk his neck for a three thousand dollar hold-up?"

Harmas stared at him for a long moment.

"Yeah ... that's a point. Look, let's keep an open mind on this. The Barlowe woman has already lied once. Let's go and talk to her ... maybe she'll lie again."

Meg Barlowe was sitting up in bed as the nurse led Jenson and Harmas into her room. Although her left eye was still badly bruised, Harmas was again aware of her sensual handsomeness.

"I have to worry you again, Mrs Barlowe," Jenson said. "I'm told you'll be leaving here in a couple of days."

Meg looked from Jenson to Harmas and then back to Jenson again.

"Yes."

Harmas had an idea she was nervous. He stood back and watched her.

"I understand you and your husband spent the evening at the Court roadhouse and he then persuaded you to go with him to Jason's Glen. Is that correct?" Jenson asked.

Meg nodded.

"Yes."

"Did you want to go with him?"

"Not particularly. In fact I told him it mightn't be safe, but he laughed at me. I guess he was a little high ... I guess I was too."

"It was his idea to go out there ... not yours?"

She stared at him for a long moment before saying, "That's right."

"When you reached Jason's Glen, did you see anyone up there ... any parked car?"

"No. I – I thought we had the place to ourselves."

"How long were you there before the attack started?"

"About five minutes ... a little more."

"What happened exactly?"

"We were talking. Then suddenly I saw a flash and heard a bang. Phil ... fell forward. I looked around and there was this man. He pointed the gun at me and told me to get out of the car. I got out and started to run. Although he was short and fat, he was very quick. He caught up with me and jerked me around. I struck him and his hat fell off. I saw he was completely bald."

"You are sure of that?" Jenson asked. "He couldn't have been very fair or even white haired, and in the moonlight, you thought he was bald?"

"No ... he had no hair at all."

"If you saw him again, would you be able to identify him?"

"Oh, yes ... I'm sure of that."

"Then what happened?"

"We struggled. He hit me on the side of my face with the barrel of the gun." She looked down at her tightly clenched hands. "After a while, I came to and found I was ... half undressed and my face was hurting. He had gone. I went over to the car. I touched Phil. I knew he was dead. I couldn't get him out of the driving seat. I walked down the road to the highway. I kept falling. It took me a long time. Finally, I got there and then ... well, next thing I remember is coming to in this room."

Harmas moved forward and Jenson, taking the hint stepped back.

"Mrs Barlowe, ten days ago your husband insured himself for fifty thousand dollars," Harmas said with his friendly, charming smile. "You must forgive me if I ask a few questions. I am an insurance investigator. When someone insures himself for such a sum and then suddenly dies, investigations must be made. You understand that?"

Meg stared suspiciously at him.

"I don't know," she said. "All I know is that I have lost my husband."

"You were very fond of him?"

"Of course ... but what's that to you?"

"Isn't it a fact, Mrs Barlowe that you and your husband no longer lived together as man and wife?"

Meg looked at Jenson; her cobalt-blue eyes suddenly as hard as glass.

"Tell this smart boy to lay off," she said. "You know as well as I do, I don't have to answer those kind of questions."

"You're quite right," Harmas said quickly. "You don't, but it's my job, unfortunately, to ask them." There was a pause as she stared defiantly at him, then he said, "I understand your husband was a crack pistol shot. Did he have his gun with him when you and he went to Jason's Glen?"

Meg stiffened.

"No ... of course not."

"He never carried his gun around with him?"

She closed her eyes.

"I don't know."

"His gun is at home?"

Her eyes flicked open.

"I don't understand. What has Phil's gun got to do with all this?"

Harmas smiled again, shrugging his shoulders.

"Nothing or something. He kept his gun at home?"

There was a long pause, then she said, "He got rid of it. He hasn't done any shooting for a long time. He gave the gun away."

Jenson was now interested.

"Who did he give it to?" he asked sharply.

Meg hesitated, then shook her head.

"I don't know. He told me he had got rid of it. He might have sold it ... I don't know."

"When was this?" Harmas asked.

"I don't remember ... sometime ago."

"Three weeks ... six months?"

Again she hesitated before saying, "I think about nine months ... soon after we married."

As Jenson was about to say something, Harmas said quickly, "Well, thanks, Mrs Barlowe. We won't worry you further. I hope you make a quick recovery."

He put his hand on Jenson's arm and steered him to the door.

Meg watched them go. Her heart was thumping and there was a sick feeling of fear growing like a hot coil inside her.

As Jenson and Harmas walked down the corridor, Harmas said, "Don't let's rush this, Fred. Our next move is to find her boyfriend. Come back with me to the hotel and I'll give you her dossier."

"Just because she happens to have a record," Jenson said heavily, "it doesn't mean she murdered her husband."

Harmas grinned at him.

"Maddox would love that remark. If you go on making those bright deductions, you'll finish up as Chief of Police." As he got into the car beside Jenson, he went on, "Hey! Here's an idea! If she has a boyfriend, guess which room in Barlowe's house he is most likely to visit?"

Jenson started the car.

"Go on ... I can guess."

"The way she keeps that house, never cleaning it, you might find his fingerprints. Why not send your boys out there and go over the bedroom before she leaves hospital? You could do it nice and quiet without anyone knowing. If she has a record, he might too and then we could find him a lot faster than waiting for him to come out from under the wraps. And another thing ... fingerprint the gun box. You might get a surprise there."

Jensen drove in silence to the hotel, frowning, then as he pulled up outside the hotel he said, "Yeah, you've got something. Okay, I'll send the boys out there this afternoon."

"Who runs the Pru Town Small Arms Club?" Harmas asked as he got out of the car, "and where do I find him?"

"Harry Seamore. You'll probably find him at the club on Sycamore Street. Why?"

"I want to talk to him," Harmas said. "Stick around, I'll get the dossier."

Harry Seamore, a heavy built, red-faced man in his early forties, shook hands with Harmas after Harmas had introduced himself.

"I'm interested in Barlowe's gun," Harmas said. "I've been told he gave the gun away about nine months ago. Do you know who he gave it to?"

Seamore, settling in his chair, looked puzzled.

"I think you have made a mistake. Phil wouldn't ever give his guns away. I know for a fact he had one of them last week. I happened to have borrowed it from him."

Harmas leaned forward.

"Guns? Did he have more than one?"

Seamore grinned.

"He had a pair and they were beauties. I ought to know. I got them for him: they were a matched pair: about the best .38s I've ever handled."

Harmas ran his fingers through his hair as he frowned at Seamore.

"You just said you borrowed one of his guns?"

"That's right. A friend of mine from Miami was staying with me. He reckons he is a pretty good shot." Seamore's pleasant face creased again into a smile. "We had a wager. I use a .45, but my friend is used to a .38 and he hadn't his gun with him. So I called Phil and asked him if he'd lend me one of his guns. My friend and I had this match ... he using Phil's gun. I returned the gun to Phil three days before the poor guy was killed."

Harmas leaned back in his chair until the chair back creaked.

"Where did this match take place, Mr Seamore?"

"Right here," Seamore said, jerking his thumb towards the window through which Harmas could see a shooting alley. "We set up two target boxes and we both fired fifteen rounds. I pipped my friend by an inner."

"What are the chances of getting the spent bullets from both guns, Mr Seamore?" Harmas asked.

"Easiest thing in the world. There's been no shooting for the past week. The slugs are in the boxes right now."

"You know which box your friend shot into?"

" 'Of course."

"Could I use your telephone?"

"Go right ahead."

Smiling happily, Harmas dialled police headquarters.

11

Anson had two likely prospects to call on in Pru Town. He then planned to spend the night at the Marlborough Hotel before returning to Brent.

As he drove along the busy highway, he wondered what was happening to Meg. She would soon be discharged from hospital. He had already warned her to destroy the insurance policy he had given to Barlowe. This he was sure she had done. He had sent the policy for a claim of $50,000, signed by Barlowe to Jack Jameson, a young but alert lawyer who was now acting for Meg.

Not for one moment had Anson any misgivings that his plans weren't foolproof. The police would be hunting for the bald-headed sex maniac. The press was sympathetic towards Meg. Jameson would put in the claim and Maddox would have to meet it. There was, however, one slight uneasiness in Anson's mind ... this dossier Harmas had mentioned. Anson kept asking himself what could be in it.

His two calls successfully completed, he drove back to the hotel. It was after he had finished his lunch and was walking towards the exit when he ran into Harmas.

"There you are," Harmas said. "I was hoping to see you. I want to talk to you."

Anson looked sharply at him, then followed him into the deserted lounge. They sat in a far corner.

"What is it?" Anson said, waving to the waiter to bring coffee.

"The Barlowe affair," Harmas said. "Maddox is right. That man kills me! He is always right. The claim is phoney."

Anson took from his pocket a pack of cigarettes. He offered it and the two men lit up.

"Go on ... tell me," he said, his voice steady and wooden.

The waiter brought them coffee. When he had gone, Harmas said, "I'm sure as I'm sitting here this woman, with the help of a boyfriend, murdered her husband. They used the sex killer as a front."

Anson stared at the burning end of his cigarette. Don't panic, he told himself. What has he found out? What have I done wrong? He remembered with a feeling of relief that he had an unbreakable alibi.

"You don't really expect me to believe this, do you?" he said. "Isn't this something Maddox has cooked up to get out of settling the claim?"

"No," Harmas said quietly. "I have seen her dossier ... you haven't. She is capable of anything. I'm sure Maddox is right as he always is."

Anson's mouth became too dry for smoking. He crushed out his cigarette.

"What's in this dossier, then?"

"The woman has a jail record," Harmas said. "She has been a prostitute. The Tracing Agency says she became infatuated with a man who lived with her. They don't know who this guy is, but she turned thief to keep him and got a three months' sentence. When she came out of jail, her pimp had disappeared. She met Barlowe. It's an odd thing how someone like Barlowe ... a mean-tempered, middle-aged man ... does fall for a tart. He fell for her, and they married. It's my guess she met her pimp again, and together they cooked up this idea of getting Barlowe to insure himself and then the two of them knocked him off."

His face expressionless, Anson said, "Can you prove any of this?"

"I have some proof. Okay, I admit it wouldn't stand up in court, but it is enough to make Maddox fight every inch of the way before we pay her claim."

Anson leaned back in his chair.

"She is a client of mine. You don't seem to realise how tricky this is for me. The word gets around. Mrs Barlowe is front-page news. People are sorry for her. The newspapers have made a big play about her being raped and her husband being killed. If Maddox fights her claim, where do I stand? Don't you see the situation I'm in? Every time I call on a prospect to try to sell him a life policy, he'll say, 'What's the use? If anything happens to me, your people won't settle ... look at the Barlowe case.' Can't you see that?"

"Sure," Harmas said, "but you're not suggesting that we pay out on a phoney claim, are you?"

"Is it phoney? Just because you've found out this woman has a police record, does that make her a murderess? What proof have you got?"

"I've caught her out in two lies," Harmas said. "It was she who persuaded Barlowe to go out to Jason's Glen and I have a witness who'll swear to it, but she claims it was Barlowe who wanted to go ... to be romantic. I have proof they slept alone. Barlowe wasn't the romantic type ... he was a pervert. It's my bet that her boyfriend was waiting at the Glen for them. There's a telephone record at the roadhouse where they spent the evening that a call was put through to a call box near the glen. I can't prove she actually made the call, but it certainly looks as if she did. I think she was alerting her boyfriend that she and Barlowe were on the way to the glen."

"Pretty circumstantial, isn't it?" Anson asked, staring at Harmas.

"Oh sure, but it turns on the red light. There's an impression of a car tyre by the call box and we found the same impression up at the Glen. If we find her boyfriend has a tyre that matched the impression, he'll have a lot of explaining to do."

Anson kept his face expressionless, but there was a sudden chill around his heart.

"The impression could have been made any time, couldn't it? What else have you got?"

Harmas sat forward.

"This is the topper," he said. "Barlowe was a crack pistol shot: he owned two guns; .38s. Both these guns are missing. Mrs Barlowe told us Barlowe had given one gun away, but Harry Seamore, the secretary of the Target Club, is certain, Barlowe would never have parted with these guns. Now there's something ... Barlowe was shot with his own gun. We have been able to check the slugs. And here's something really sensational; the same guy that killed Barlowe, killed the cop in the Caltex hold-up. How do you like that?"

"You've certainly been busy," Anson said as he bent to adjust his shoe string. He felt he had lost colour and he cursed himself for using Barlowe's gun. At the time it had seemed so easy and convenient ... what blind spot had led him into making such a stupid, dangerous mistake? He straightened. "What does Lieutenant Jenson think ... does he think Barlowe did that hold-up? Could explain how he got hold of the money to pay for his premium. Come to think of it, it could be the answer. He was desperate to start up on his own. He probably hadn't the money to pay for the premium and staged this hold-up. Could explain why he paid up in cash."

Harmas stroked his nose.

"Yeah; you have an idea. All the same, I'm still convinced Mrs Barlowe has a boyfriend and he and she cooked up Barlowe's murder."

"Just who is this boyfriend you keep talking about?" Anson demanded.

"We're looking for him. He shouldn't be all that hard to turn up." Harmas finished his coffee. "Well, that puts you in the picture. I'm alerting Maddox. He'll love it! I don't think Mrs Barlowe is going to get paid. She could end up in the gas chamber."

Anson got to his feet.

"You have still to prove it," he said. "Until you do prove it, I'm going along with my client. This kind of situation could put me right out of business here. See you," and he walked out of the lounge.

Harmas watched him go, a sudden, puzzled expression in his alert grey eyes.

Harmas had just finished breakfast and had moved into the lounge of the hotel to read the newspapers when Jenson came striding in.

"That fingerprint idea of yours has paid off," Jenson said. "I think we're on to her boyfriend. There are two sets of men's prints in her bedroom. One set we have no record of, but the other belongs to a guy named Sailor Hogan. He was one time light heavyweight champion of California and he lived in Los Angeles. He works now in Brent for Joe Duncan, a bookmaker. As Hogan lived in LA and Mrs

163

Barlowe worked there as a prostitute could be he was her pimp."

"Get any prints from the gun-box?" Harmas asked.

"Yeah, but they aren't Hogan's; they belong to the other guy," Jenson told him. "I'm going to talk to Hogan now. Do you want to come?"

Harmas climbed to his feet.

"I'd like to see you stop me," he said.

Sailor Hogan lounged back in his chair, a sneering grin on his battle-scarred face.

"Look, fellows, snap it up," he said. "I have things to do. What's biting you?"

"Where were you on the night of September 21st?" Jenson demanded.

Hogan's grin widened.

"What's this? What am I supposed to have been doing?"

"What were you doing and where were you?"

"I don't know," Hogan said, shrugging. "That's over two weeks ago, isn't it?"

"Think about it," Jenson said with his cop voice. "You could be in trouble. Better think hard."

"Well, if it's like that," Hogan said, still grinning, "maybe I can do something about it." He took from his pocket a slim red diary and began to flick through the pages. "September 21st?"

"You heard me!" Jenson snapped.

"Well, now yeah ... just as well I keep a diary, isn't it?" Hogan looked at Harmas and winked. "I've been in a spot of trouble in the past, now I always keep a record. Comes in useful when the law gets nosy."

"Come on, Hogan!" Jenson barked. "What were you doing?"

"I was in Lambsville ... I had a job to do for Joe Duncan ... any particular time bothering you?"

"Three to four o'clock in the morning."

"Well, for Pete's sake. I was in bed! Where else would I be?"

"Can you prove it?"

Hogan leered.

"Easiest thing in the world, Lieutenant. I don't often sleep alone. I get scared of the dark. I had a babe to look after me." His sneering grin widened. "She has a reason to remember. You ask her ... Kit Litman. She works at the Casino Club."

"What were you doing on the night of September 30th?"

Hogan again winked at Harmas as he flicked pages in his diary.

"Time?" he asked.

"Between nine and eleven p.m."

"That's an easy one," Hogan said. "I was playing poker with four of my pals. We played from eight to midnight at Sam's bar. Check if you don't believe me. I was with Joe Gershwin, Ted Macklin, Frankie Stewart and Jack Hammond." He lolled at ease in his chair. "They'll tell you. We started play at eight and finished at around two o'clock. Is that all? I have work to do. You can't pin anything on me, Lieutenant. I keep my nose clean."

Jenson asked abruptly, "You know Mrs Barlowe?" Hogan was waiting for this question.

"I can't say I do ... have I missed anything?"

"You know Philip Barlowe?"

"The guy who was knocked off? No ... what's all this in aid of?"

"Have you ever been to the Barlowe house?"

165

Hogan's smile began to fade. He didn't like the cold, hard stare Jenson was giving him.

"Is it likely?"

"How does it happen then your fingerprints were found in the Barlowe house?" Jenson demanded, leaning forward.

For a moment Hogan gaped at him, then he forced a rueful grin.

"You coppers! You been out there getting fingerprints?"

"We have yours Hogan," Jenson said. "Let's start again; do you know Meg Barlowe?"

Hogan shrugged.

"Oh, sure. What's it matter now Barlowe's dead? She and I used to go around together before she married Barlowe. We met again and she invited me out there from time to time. Barlowe hadn't what it takes!" He had recovered his nerve and he winked at Harmas as he went on, "I was just protecting the lady's honour. But since you know, well, there it is. Anything else you want to know?"

"There's another set of prints in the house," Jenson said. "A man ... know who it could be?"

Hogan picked a tooth with a dirty fingernail.

"You surprise me," he said. "I thought I was the only one. I wouldn't know ... why not ask her?"

Jenson looked at Harmas and shrugged. This gesture was an admission of defeat.

"Where's your car?" Jenson asked.

"Outside ... the blue Buick."

The two men left the apartment, and as they shut the door, Hogan gave a sneering little laugh.

It took Jenson only a few minutes to satisfy himself that Hogan's car hadn't made the tyre track at Jason's Glen. He looked in disgust at Harmas.

"Well, that's it," he said. "There's another boyfriend. Hogan couldn't have done it. I'll check his alibi, but I know him ... his alibis stick."

"So we start looking for the other boyfriend," Harmas said.

"That's it," Jenson said. "I'll turn the screws on this woman."

"Not yet," Harmas said. "I have an idea I'd like to work on first. When we do start working on her, we want enough facts to crack her."

Anson drove his car into the Shell Service station on the Brent highway.

The manager of the Station, Jack Hornby, came out to shake hands.

"Jack," Anson said, "I'm worried about my tyres. I don't like them. I want Firestone fitted. Will you fix it?"

"Happy to do it, Mr Anson," Hornby said. He walked around Anson's car. "I don't see why you should be worried about this lot. Could run another 8,000 miles."

"A pal of mine had a burst with one of these. Fit me with Firestone."

"Okay; I can give you discount on your old tyres if you like?"

"Thanks, but I'll take them. Put them in the trunk. I'll wait. How long will it take?"

"Best part of an hour," Hornby said, looking puzzled. "I can lend you a car, Mr Anson and I'll send ..."

"I'll wait," Anson said curtly.

Edwin Merryweather, the manager of the Pru Town National Bank, was short, fat and fussily old-fashioned. He wore a neat, well pressed blue suit and a polka dot bow tie.

As Harmas shook hands with him, Harmas thought he looked like a character out of a novel by Sinclair Lewis.

"I understand Mr Philip Barlowe was a client of yours?" Harmas said after he had introduced himself. "We are expecting a claim to be made against us. Mr Barlowe took out a life coverage with us a few days before he died. We have to check on certain points before we meet the claim."

Merryweather lifted his eyebrows.

"Yes?"

"Did Mr Barlowe consult you about this policy?"

Merryweather regarded his nicely polished fingernails before saying, "As it happens ... he did."

"I understand he took out the policy as security for a bank loan. Is that correct?"

"Those were his intentions."

"Did he tell you how much he planned to borrow?"

"Three thousand dollars. We would have been happy to have advanced him that amount if he had lodged his policy with us."

Harmas became alert.

"I understand Mr Barlowe wanted a much larger sum than three thousand dollars."

Merryweather looked prim.

"We couldn't advance him any more than that sum on a five thousand dollar policy."

"Five thousand? Barlowe was insured for fifty thousand dollars!"

Merryweather looked startled.

"Surely not. Are you sure there isn't a mistake?" Looking at Harmas' set expression, he frowned and paused to adjust his bow tie. "No, obviously you would know. Mr Barlowe told me he was arranging to insure his life for five thousand dollars and as your company offered a five per cent discount for cash, he wanted to pay the first premium in cash. He drew out practically all the money he had in his account to meet the premium."

Harmas felt a prickle of excitement run up his spine. Now he really was on to something, he told himself.

Quietly, he said, "I don't understand. We don't give discount for cash ... what made him say that?"

"Mr Barlowe told me that your representative gave him this information ... someone ... I think ... it's Mr Anson, isn't it?"

"He's our representative," Harmas said slowly. "But there is obviously some mistake here. How much did Barlowe draw out of his account?"

"A hundred and fifty dollars."

Harmas rubbed the back of his neck; the amount needed to cover a five thousand dollar life policy.

"There's something odd about all this. Barlowe took out a fifty thousand dollar coverage and he paid the first premium in cash! One thousand-odd dollars."

"I can't imagine where he got that amount from, Mr Harmas. He was often overdrawn."

Harmas thought for a long moment, then he got to his feet.

"Well, thanks for your time."

Merryweather made a gesture with his fat hands.

"Only too happy to be of service," he said.

As Harmas picked up his key at the reception desk, Tom Nodley said, "There's a woman wanting to talk to you, Mr Harmas. She's been waiting some time in the bar."

The smirking expression on Nodley's face made Harmas stare sharply at him.

"Who is she?"

"Her name is Fay Lawley," Nodley leaned forward, lowering his voice. "She's one of the girls." He winked. "I can get rid of her for you, Mr Harmas, if you don't want to see her."

"I always see everyone," Harmas said and walked across the lobby to the bar.

He spotted Fay sitting in a corner, nursing a whisky and water, and he joined her.

She smiled at him.

"Come and sit down. I've been trying to contact you for days."

"Is that a fact," Harmas said. He signalled to the waiter, then sat down opposite her. "I've been busy. You know me ... I don't know you."

The waiter came over and Harmas ordered a Scotch on the rocks.

"I'm Fay Lawley," she said. "I live around here." Her painted lips twisted into a hard little smile. "You're with National Fidelity, aren't you?"

"That's right."

"Well, I thought you'd like some information."

The waiter came over with Harmas' drink.

"I thrive on information," Harmas said when the waiter had gone away. He offered cigarettes. They both lit up. "What is this ... some kind of deal?"

Fay shook her head.

"I'm just paying off a grudge. Treat me nice and I'm lovely. Treat me rough and I'm the original stinker. I'll do anything for a man who is decent, but the jerk who tries to shove me around gets his throat cut."

"Should this interest me?" Harmas asked, looking at her intently.

"I don't know ... you're an insurance cop, aren't you?"

170

"That's it."

"Would you be interested in the way your salesmen act?"
Harmas sipped his drink.

"Why, sure ... any particular salesman?"

"A little runt ... Johnny Anson."

Harmas put down his drink. He kept his face expressionless.

"What about him?"

Her face suddenly vicious, her eyes glittering, Fay leaned forward and began to talk.

12

It was Harmas' idea, and as soon as he put it to Jenson, the Lieutenant agreed.

"Mrs Barlowe will be returning home tomorrow," Harmas said, "this is our last chance. Let's go out there and really look the place over. Okay, your fingerprint boys have gone over the place, but now let us go over it together?"

"Just what are we looking for?" Jenson asked as he got into his car.

"The guns. They could be hidden somewhere in the house. They bother me."

Arriving at the house soon after midday, Harmas and Jenson got out of the car and surveyed the garden.

"You know, Barlowe had genius," Harmas said. "It's odd, isn't it, how this kind of talent and artistic ability can go hand in hand with rottenness."

Jenson wasn't interested. He grunted and then walked over to the front door. He had no difficulty in slipping the lock. The two men wandered into the lobby. The stale smell of stuffiness and dirt made them wrinkle their noses.

"Let's go and look at Barlowe's bedroom first," Harmas said and led the way up the stairs.

Systematically, the two men searched the room. It was while Jenson was grimacing with disgust at a pack of photographs he had unearthed, that Harmas, pushing aside the bed, found one of the floorboards loose.

Taking out his pocket knife, he carefully lifted the board and shot his flashlight beam into the cavity.

"Here it is," he said, "and what the devil's this?"

Jenson peered over his shoulder at the .38 automatic that lay on the plaster. Harmas fished out a white bathing cap and two rubber cheek pads. Jenson inserted a pencil into the barrel of the gun and lifted it carefully from its hiding place.

Harmas was staring with interest at the bathing cap.

"The bald-headed man," he said and looked at Jenson. "It jells. All this muck ... now this ... I'll bet a hundred bucks that this is the Glyn Hill murder weapon."

Jenson stroked his thick nose.

"Yeah? I never throw money away. Well, come on, now we're here, let's look at the rest of this hole."

They remained in the stuffy little house all the afternoon, but they didn't find the other gun. Jenson had called police headquarters and a couple of cars, loaded with technical men, had arrived. Two of them had taken the .38 down to the Ballistics department at Brent. By the time Jenson and Harmas had returned to Brent, the experts were able to tell them that the gun was the Glyn Hill murder weapon.

Anson was sensitive to atmosphere.

When Harmas walked into the office soon after six o'clock and just when Anson was preparing to go home he was immediately aware that Harmas was hostile.

Harmas came abruptly to the reason of his visit. He described his interview with Merryweather, his grey, steady eyes probing and suspicious.

When Harmas had finished talking, Anson said, "I can't imagine what he means. I never offered Barlowe a five per

173

cent discount. Why should I? Are you sure Merryweather has his facts right?"

"I'm not sure about anything," Harmas said in a tone that belied his words. "Barlowe told him you told Barlowe if he paid the first premium in cash, we would give him a five per cent discount. What's more, he drew out one hundred and fifty dollars from his account to cover his first premium ... nearly every dollar he owned."

Anson picked up a pencil and began to draw aimless designs on his blotter.

"The premium was twelve twenty two," he said, without looking at Harmas. "Some mistake here."

"Originally, Barlowe intended to take out a five thousand dollar policy," Harmas said. "Merryweather is certain of that. Barlowe only wanted to borrow three thousand dollars."

Anson shifted uneasily. He paused for a moment while he lit a cigarette.

"All I can tell you," he said finally, "is that Barlowe filled in one of your coupon enquiries. When I called on him, he asked for a fifty thousand dollar policy ... you've seen the policy ... it was signed by him! He might have talked the deal over with Merryweather before he saw me. When he got home and thought about it, he must have decided to go for the bigger policy."

"Ten times as big?" Harmas said quietly, "where did the money come from to pay for such a premium?"

"He had the money ... he gave it to me," Anson said.

"Could I see the inquiry form?" Harmas asked. "I would like to be sure we have proof, that Barlowe talked to Merryweather before he saw you."

Anson stiffened. The ash from his cigarette fell into his lap.

"I destroyed it," he said.

Harmas now paused to light a cigarette. He stared probingly at Anson who forced himself to stare back.

"Do you usually destroy your coupons?" Harmas asked.

"Only when I have made a sale. As I sold Barlowe a policy there was no point in keeping the coupon."

Harmas considered this, then shrugged.

"Yeah ... I see that." He let smoke drift from his nostrils for a long moment, then suddenly leaning forward, he asked, "Just for the record ... where were you on the night of September 30th?"

Anson felt a sudden cold stab of fear go through him.

"What do you mean?"

Harmas smiled.

"You know Maddox. He loves alibis. He wants to know where everyone was, remotely connected with Barlowe on the night of his death," Harmas' smile broadened. "It wouldn't surprise me if he doesn't ask me for an alibi as well. It doesn't mean a thing and if I'm treading on thin ice say so and we'll skip it."

"Of course not."

Anson opened a drawer in his desk and took out an engagement diary.

"I was working late, right here," he said in a cold, flat voice. "I didn't leave here until eleven. The janitor downstairs will tell you if you want to check."

"Relax," Harmas said, waving his hands. "I don't want to check." He leaned back in his chair. "You know, I've been thinking about this case. I'm inclined to agree with you. Even if this woman isn't on the level, it might be wiser to pay her. As you say, in this district, we might easily lose a lot of business by fighting her claim. Maddox is coming

175

here this evening. I'm going to try to talk him into paying up."

Anson stiffened and leaned forward.

"Maddox is coming here?"

"Yeah. He wants to talk to Jenson. I'll let you know if I persuade him to meet the claim. Will you be home tonight?"

Anson nodded.

"Up to around nine o'clock, but I know Maddox; he won't pay up."

"He could do. Old man Burrows doesn't like bad publicity. The newspapers could have a go at us. I'll see what I can do." Harmas pushed back his chair. "Getting away from business, do you know anything about that antique shop at the corner of the block? I picked up a paperweight there. They swore it was a genuine antique." He took from his pocket a plastic bag and slid out an ornate glass paperweight. He pushed it across the desk towards Anson. "Helen is nuts about antiques, but I am now wondering if it is a fake ... could be Japanese, 1960!"

Without thinking, Anson picked up the paperweight and examined it, then he shrugged.

"I don't know; looks nice. If you tell her it's a hundred years old, she'll be happy."

He handed the paperweight back and Harmas carefully returned it to its plastic bag.

"Yeah: you have something there." He stood up. "If I can talk Maddox into paying up, I'll call you. So long for now."

When Harmas had gone, Anson lit a cigarette and stared thoughtfully at the opposite wall. He had an uneasy feeling that this murder plan of his was slowly coming unstuck at the seams. He tried to assure himself that although the situation was tricky, it wasn't dangerous. Not for one moment did he believe that Maddox would pay up now. He was sure that the insurance money was as good as lost. What he had to be careful about was not to be involved. It was Meg's fault, of course. If she hadn't told him all those lies about her past life, he wouldn't be in this spot now.

He was still sitting at his desk, probing the situation, still wondering if he had made some fatal mistake, when some thirty minutes later, there came a gentle tap on his door.

"Come on in," he called.

The door opened and Jud Jones, the night guard wandered in.

Surprised, Anson stared at him.

"Hello, Jud," he said. "I was just going home. Is there something I can do for you?"

Jones moved his fat body further into the office. He closed the door. There was an uneasy, smirking expression on his face Anson hadn't seen before and which he didn't like.

"I wanted a word with you, Mr Anson," he said.

"Can't it wait?" Anson said a little impatiently. "I want to get home."

Jones shook his head.

"I guess not, Mr Anson. This is important ... to you as well as to me."

Anson moved over to the window so his back was to the fading light.

"Go ahead ... what is it?"

"This guy Harmas ... you know him?"

Anson's hands turned into fists.

"Yes ... what about him?"

"He has been asking questions about you, Mr Anson."

With an effort, Anson kept his face expressionless. So Harmas had checked his alibi. Well, that would get him nowhere.

Forcing his voice to sound natural, Anson said, "I know all about that. It's to do with this murder case. The police want to check everyone's alibi; everyone remotely connected with Barlowe. I happened to have sold Barlowe an insurance policy so I'm involved. It's just routine. Don't let it worry you."

Jones took a half smoked cigarette from behind his ear, stuck it on his lower lip and set fire to it.

"It's not worrying me, Mr Anson. I thought it might be worrying you. You see, I told him you were right here in this office between nine and eleven. I told him you were using the typewriter."

There was a sneering tone in his voice that made Anson's eyes move intently over the fat, sly face.

"That's right," he said. "I told him the same thing. Just as well I didn't have company that night, isn't it?" He forced a smile.

"Yeah," Jones said without returning Anson's smile. "Well, I told him you were here, but he's only a private dick. What if the cops should ask me?"

"You tell them the same thing, Jud," Anson said, his voice sharpening.

"You can't expect me to tell lies to the cops, Mr Anson," Jones said, shaking his head. "I can't afford to get into trouble ... they could make me an accessory ..."

Anson felt a chill growing around his heart.

"What do you mean? Accessory? What are you talking about?"

"You weren't in your office that night, Mr Anson."

Anson sat abruptly on the edge of his desk. His legs felt as if they wouldn't support him.

"What makes you say that?" he asked, his voice husky.

Jones dropped his cigarette butt on the floor and trod on it.

"I had run out of cigarettes," he said. "I thought I might borrow a couple from you. I knocked on the door. No one answered, but the typewriter kept going. I knocked again, then I thought something must be wrong. I opened the door with my pass key. You weren't there, Mr Anson. There was a tape recorder playing back the sound of a typewriter working and very realistic it sounded ... it had me completely fooled."

Anson felt cold sweat run from his armpits down his ribs.

Sunk! he thought, now what am I going to do?

His immediate impulse was to take Barlowe's gun from the locked drawer in his desk and murder Jones. The thought was scarcely in his mind before he dismissed it. He would never have the strength to move this great hulk of a body from his office once Jones was dead. He had to gain time to think.

"That's right, Jud," he said. "I wasn't in my office but I had nothing to do with the murder ... nothing at all."

Jones, who had been watching Anson closely, smirked. Anson could smell the sweat of excitement and fear coming from the fat man.

"I'm sure, Mr Anson ... never crossed my mind you did have anything to do with it. I just thought I'd better let you know if the cops asked me. I'll have to tell them the truth." He cocked his head on one side, and went on, "it wouldn't do any harm, would it, Mr Anson?"

Anson said slowly, "Well, Jud, it might."

Jones managed to look sad.

"I wouldn't like that. You've always been good to me. What sort of harm would it do?"

"I could lose my job," Anson said. "I set up this alibi because I was fooling around with a married woman and her husband is on to me. I wanted to prove I was right here instead of being with her." Even to him, this sounded pretty feeble, but he had no time to think up something better.

"Is that right?" Jud said and leered. "You were always sharp with girls." He paused to scratch the back of his fat neck. "Well, maybe I could forget it if that's all it is. Maybe I could ... I'll have to think about it."

Anson smelling blackmail, said quickly ... too quickly, "If a hundred dollars would be of any use to you, Jud ... after all, although I have nothing to do with it, this is a murder inquiry. How about a hundred bucks and you keep me in the clear?"

Jones lolled his massive frame against the wall.

"Well, I don't know, Mr Anson. It worries me. To tell the truth, my wife is far from well. The doc says she should go away. The climate here doesn't seem to agree with her. Moving is an expensive business. You couldn't run to a thousand, could you? For that I'll forget everything and you will be doing us a good turn."

Anson suddenly became calm. He realised the situation. He told himself he would have to kill this fat, hulking blackmailer, but he would have to stall him until he got him where he could kill him in safety.

"A thousand!" he exclaimed. "For Pete's sake, Jud! Where do you imagine I'd find that kind of money? Two hundred is the best I could do."

Jones shook his head. His expression became more sorrowful. "I'd like to help you, Mr Anson, but suppose the cops found out I had lied to them? What would happen to my wife? They could put me away for a couple of years. Two hundred bucks is no good to me."

Anson stared at the fat, sweating blackmailer for a long moment, then he said, "Give me a little time; two or three days. I might manage to find five hundred, but that would be the top. How about that?"

"I hate to press a guy as nice as you, Mr Anson," Jones said and Anson was quick to detect a hardening in the expression of his eyes. "It'll have to be a thousand or nothing. I will give you a couple of days to decide."

Anson watched him heave his bulk away from the wall and over to the door. As Jones opened the door, he paused and leered at Anson.

"My wife knows," he said. "I never keep anything from her, but she can keep her mouth shut as well as I can. Good night, Mr Anson."

He went out into the corridor and closed the door after him.

On his way back to his apartment, Anson stopped off at the Shell Service Station. Hornby shook hands with him and asked him how he liked his new tyres.

"They're fine," Anson said. "I looked in to settle the account."

"Thanks, Mr Anson. Come into the office and I'll give you a receipt."

As Hornby began to write out the receipt, he said casually, "The police have been asking about your old set of tyres, Mr Anson."

Anson was looking at a tyre pressure chart, hanging on the wall. His back was to Hornby. He felt the shock of Hornby's words like a physical blow.

Without turning, he asked, "The police? Why?"

"Something to do with the Barlowe murder," Hornby said. "It seems the killer left an imprint of his tyres on the murder spot. The police are checking on everyone who has changed his tyres recently. I told them that you had changed your tyres and that you took your old set away."

Now the first shock was over, Anson turned.

"That's okay," he said. "I'll see Lieutenant Jenson. He's a good friend of mine ... I wouldn't like him to think I had anything to do with the murder," and he forced a laugh.

"I just thought I'd mention it," Hornby said, giving Anson the receipt.

"Sure ... I'll see the Lieutenant."

As Anson drove away from the garage, he had a feeling he was in a trap. How many more mistakes was he going to make? He had been so eager to get the insurance money, he had rushed into this thing. He had been crazy to have used Barlowe's gun. He had been even more crazy to have been so damned careless as to get a garage that knew him to change his tyres. Then there was Harmas asking about the coupon enquiry form and worse still, he now had no alibi for the night when Barlowe died!

Could this bright idea of his be slowly but surely collapsing? He mustn't lose his nerve, he told himself. So long as his alibi stood up, he was in the clear. What was he to do about Jones? His hands turned damp as he gripped the steering wheel. Would he have to murder both Jones and his wife? Somehow he would have to silence them. He was sure, even if he did manage to find one thousand dollars, Jones would come back for more. This tyre business ... he had dumped his old set in a breakdown yard among hundreds of other used tyres. No one had seen him do it. Suppose Jones did betray him? Could the police prove he murdered Barlowe? He didn't think they could ... unless

Meg's nerve broke. If they worked on her, she might involve him.

She would be back the following night and alone in the sordid dirty, little house. He would go out there late and talk to her.

Maddox flicked cigarette ash off his tie.

"I never liked Anson," he said. "There has always been something queer about him. He looks sexually starved and when a man looks like that, I don't like him."

Lieutenant Jenson sat behind his desk. Astride a chair, Harmas kept his eyes on Maddox. They had spent the past hour going over the details that Jenson and Harmas had collected covering Anson's connection with Barlowe's murder.

"Let's take another look at it," Maddox said, dropping his cigarette butt on the floor and lighting another cigarette. "We know Anson has been in this woman's bedroom. We know also he has handled Barlowe's gun-box. You have his fingerprints in the bedroom and on the gun-box. We know this because you got his prints on the glass paperweight." He looked approvingly at Harmas. "That was smart." He drew in a lungful of smoke and let it drift down his thick nostrils. "We know from this woman, Fay Lawley, that Anson has been losing money on horses and has been chasing women. We know he has been living far beyond his income. We also know on the morning following the Caltex hold-up, Anson suddenly pays into his bank a thousand dollars. We know the gun that killed the officer in the hold-up belonged to Barlowe. We also know that the gun killed Barlowe. We can assume the woman gave Anson the gun. He hadn't the money to pay for the premium so it looks as if he were forced to fake the Caltex hold-up to get the

183

money and to pay off his debts to this bookmaker. We know he changed his car tyres after he was alerted by you ..." here Maddox scowled at Harmas, "that a tyre track was found on the murder spot. We also know that he has a cast-iron alibi." Maddox leaned back in his chair. "What is a cast-iron alibi? Who is this night guard who tells us Anson was working until eleven on the night Barlowe died?"

"He wouldn't stand up for three minutes under cross examination," Jenson said. "He copped a five-year stretch for blackmail ten years ago. He'd lie his mother's life away if he could earn a dollar."

Maddox ran his fingers through his hair, his red, rubbery face set in a scowl.

"Then it looks like Anson." He turned on Harmas. "What do you think? Can we nail him?"

"I don't think so," Harmas said. "We have nothing against him that a smart attorney couldn't shoot to bits. I think as you do ... I think he is our boy, but proving it is something else besides."

"Well, this is your job," Maddox said, glaring at Harmas. "So what do we do?"

Harmas smiled his slow, lazy smile.

"I think we should settle the claim. Give Mrs Barlowe fifty thousand dollars."

Maddox's face turned purple.

"Pay her! You're trying to be funny! She'll never get a dime out of me!"

Harmas glanced at his watch. It was twenty minutes to nine and he was hungry.

"I told Anson I'd persuade you to settle the claim. Just to get the right atmosphere, I think we should call her lawyer and tell him the same thing. As soon as they know the money is going to be paid out, things will start happening."

Maddox suddenly relaxed.

"Go on ... keep talking ..."

"This woman is an ex-prostitute; there is no greedier animal," Harmas said. "She won't part with any of the loot. She and Anson could have a quarrel. She'll be leaving hospital tomorrow. I thought it would be an idea to tap the telephone and plant microphones, hooked to a tape recorder around the house. It's my bet Anson will go out there as soon as he knows the money is going to be paid. We could get quite a conversation on tape."

Maddox rubbed the back of his neck as he looked at Jenson.

"The boy's smart," he said. "I won't say I can't do without him, but he makes my life a little easier than if I didn't have him." To Harmas, he said, "Go ahead ... call her lawyer and call Anson."

Anson paced up and down in his sitting-room. Every now and then, he looked impatiently at the clock on the sideboard. It was five minutes to nine o'clock. Then suddenly the telephone bell rang.

For a moment he hesitated, then picked up the receiver. It was Harmas.

"I've fixed it!" Harmas exclaimed. "Phew! I'm pretty near a wreck! Maddox has agreed to settle the claim. You have yourself to thank for it! If you hadn't been selling so much insurance in the district, Maddox would never have agreed, but even he can see that he would only be spoiling your territory if we fought the claim."

"You really mean ... there's no trick in this?"

Anson was stiff with suspicion. The idea of Maddox parting with fifty thousand dollars with the evidence he had against Meg seemed impossible.

"Don't imagine Maddox likes it," Harmas said and laughed. "He talked first on the telephone with old man Burrows. He's sure the woman fixed her husband, but he isn't sure he can prove it ... so, well, he's letting her get away with it. I've called her lawyer. He'll get the cheque tomorrow."

"Well, I'm glad," Anson said. "Thanks for calling me."

"That's okay. I thought you'd like to know. See you sometime," and Harmas hung up.

Anson slowly replaced the receiver.

Meg Barlowe stirred the fire into a blaze.

The big, dusty room gave her a feeling of security. Having Hogan, his heavy body stretched out on the settee, gave her a feeling of relaxation even though Hogan seemed in a vile mood.

The time was a few minutes after eleven p.m. Meg had left the hospital during the afternoon. As soon as she had got back to the house, she had attempted to call Hogan, but it was some hours before he answered her repeated ringing.

She had asked him to come out right away, but Hogan was busy. He said he would be around about nine o'clock, but he hadn't arrived before a few minutes after ten.

As soon as he had settled himself and had had a drink, he wanted to know when Meg was going to get the money.

"I don't know," she said helplessly. "This guy Jameson is supposed to be smart. He's put in the claim, but I haven't heard anything."

"You get after him tomorrow," Hogan snarled. "Chase him! I know lawyers. If you don't keep after them, they sit on their tails and do nothing."

Meg nodded.

"I'll get after him. What are we going to do about Anson?"

Hogan scowled at her.

"Nothing ... you give him the brush-off. What can he do? As soon as we get the money you give it to me to handle. You give him the air. You understand?"

Meg stared at him.

"I'll give you the money Jerry, but I'll also give you Anson to handle. He still has Phil's gun."

Hogan half sat up, his eyes alert. "What are you talking about?"

"I have already warned you about Anson," Meg said. "There's something about him that scares me. He's cold-blooded. It's fine for you to tell me to give him the brush off. What about me? He could do anything ... he could kill me ..."

"Yeah? He can't do a damn thing!" Hogan snarled. "Can't you see, you dope, that unless he wants to stick himself into the gas chamber, he can't do a thing? We have him over a barrel. You get the money, tell him to go to hell, and give me the money ... it's as simple as that."

"I wish it was," Meg said, clenching her fists. "You don't know him the way I do. He's ruthless. His mind is set on getting money."

Hogan swung his legs off the settee and sat up. His thick fingers closed around the buckle of his belt. With a quick movement he released the buckle and whipped the thin leather belt from around his waist.

"Okay, baby," he said, getting to his feet, "it's time you had a hiding. You're getting too big for your pants. A beating ..."

He paused as the front door bell rang. They looked at each other.

"Who's that?" Hogan said, the belt swinging idly, his eyes uneasy.

"Go and find out," Meg said. "But maybe you would like to beat me first!"

The front door bell rang, loudly and persistently.

Anson got out of his car, opened the double gates and drove the car onto the tarmac drive.

The headlights of the car lit up the garden. Before he turned off the car's headlights he saw the garden had already lost its magic neatness without Barlowe's care and discipline.

The time was half past eleven. There was a light on in the sitting-room. He paused for a moment, his hand going into his topcoat pocket. His fingers touched the cold butt of Barlowe's gun, then he walked to the front door and rang the bell.

There was no answer to his ring. He waited, aware of a cold mounting rage inside him, then he put his finger on the bell and held it there.

After a further wait, the front door was suddenly jerked open. The moonlight fell directly on Meg.

Anson remembered the first time he had seen her; in exactly the same position in which she was now standing, but now, of course, it was different. The bruise on her jaw and her slightly swollen eye marred the sensual quality she had.

At the sight of Anson, she drew in a quick, alarmed breath.

"What do you want?" she demanded. "I don't want you here ... go away!"

"Hello, Meg," Anson said with a deceptively mild smile. "We have things to talk about."

"You're not coming in!" Meg set herself to slam the door. "I have nothing to say to you!"

Anson made a quick move forward. He put his hand on her shoulder and gave her a hard shove that sent her staggering back. He entered the hall, shut the front door and then walked past her into the sitting-room.

A log fire burned cheerfully in the grate. Anson was quick to notice two half empty glasses of whisky standing on the occasional table. So she had company, he thought, and his hand slid into his pocket and touched the butt of Barlowe's gun.

As Meg followed him into the room, leaving the door open, a sudden gust of wind blew a shower of rain against the windows.

Anson moved to the fire. He looked around the room. The burning logs, the settee and the two glasses of whisky sent his mind back to the exciting moment of their first meeting. It seemed a long time ago.

"What do you want?" Meg demanded.

Anson looked searchingly at her. His eyes moved over her body. He thought: you meet a woman and she starts a chemical reaction in you. You think there is no one like her in the world, then something happens, and it is finished. She means less to me now than the used plate after a good meal, and how little can that be?

"So you had to lie to me," he said. "If you had told me you had been a tart and you had been a thief and you had

189

been in jail, I wouldn't have gone ahead with this thing, but you had to live in a dream world and lie. You hadn't the guts to tell the truth. I'm sorry for you. To me now, you are just something I find on my shoe and scrape off."

Meg hunched her shoulders. Her face was hard and her eyes bleak and indifferent. Anson knew he had no power to hurt her. Her past life had armoured her against contempt.

"Do you imagine I care what you say about me?" she said. "Get out!"

"Not just yet ... I have news for you, Meg. In spite of your record, in spite of your lies, they are going to pay the claim. You'll get the money tomorrow."

Meg stiffened, staring at him. Blood rushed to her face, then receded, leaving her pale with excitement.

"You mean that?" she demanded huskily. "You really mean they are going to pay?"

Anson waved to the telephone.

"Call Jameson. They've even told him. I talked to him before I came out here. He said he would be coming out himself tomorrow as soon as he got the cheque."

Meg drew in a long, slow breath. Watching her, Anson's face showed amused cynicism.

"We made a bargain ... remember?" he said, "I was to insure your husband and murder him and you were to share the insurance money and yourself with me. We were going away together and we were going to have a whale of a time spending fifty thousand dollars." His smile became crooked. "But now I've changed my mind. I have known too many whores to trust any of them and that now includes you. So I'll settle for half the money. Tomorrow, you will get a cheque for fifty thousand dollars. I want a cheque right now from you for twenty-five thousand dollars, and we part and I hope I never see you again."

190

Meg was aware that Hogan was just outside the room, listening to what was being said. His presence gave her the courage to say, "You get nothing! You can't force me to give you anything ... get out!"

"Don't be stupid, Meg," Anson said, his eyes bleak. "I can force you to give me my share ... make no mistake about that. You will do what I tell you or ..."

A slight movement at the door made him jerk round. His heart skipped a beat at the sight of Sailor Hogan who grinned sneeringly at him.

"Hello palsy ... you threaten me, not her. I'm more your size."

As he moved into the room, Meg backed away.

Completely taken by surprise, Anson looked blankly from Hogan to Meg and then to Hogan again. Then his quick mind realised why Hogan was here. He saw suddenly the whole fabric of the plot he had blindly walked into.

"So ... that's how it is. You and she. So you are the boyfriend the police think murdered Barlowe," he said softly. "You are the pimp from Los Angeles who they talk about."

Hogan's sneering grin widened.

"Don't get sore about it, palsy," he said, leaning his broad, fighter's shoulders against the wall. "We're all suckers at one time in our lives. The cops thought I had knocked him off, but I convinced them I didn't. I had an alibi. For your sake, I hope you have one too for they are certainly sniffing around."

"I am having half the money," Anson said, his face white, his eyes glittering. "You and your whore can have the other half, but I fixed this; I took all the risks ... so I get a half share."

Hogan laughed, slapping his thigh.

"You don't get a dime, sucker. You killed him. When Meg put up the idea, I knew we had to find a sucker in the insurance racket and so I picked you. I picked on you because I knew you were in trouble and panting for dough. I gave you the treatment, and boy, did that punch in the belly soften you up. It was that simple. All she had to do was to write that letter about insuring her jewellery and then turn the heat on." He looked over at Meg and grinned, "If she knows anything, she knows how to make a sucker out of a guy with hot pants. So you've pulled the nuts out of the fire, but don't kid yourself ... you don't get a dime. There's nothing you can do about it. You start bleating and you'll bleat yourself into the gas chamber. Get it?" Hogan winked. He jerked a thick thumb to the door. "Now, beat it. Me and my girlfriend want to be alone."

Anson remained before the fire. His eyes were intent, his mouth a thin line.

"Are you telling me it was your idea to trap me into insuring Barlowe and then murdering him?" he asked.

Hogan laughed.

"Not my idea ... she dreamed it up. You would be surprised how smart she is for a tart. I worked it, but she invented it."

Meg, listening and watching, said sharply, "You're talking too much Jerry ... shut up!"

"Let him know how it is," Hogan said, enjoying himself. "After all, he's made us fifty thousand bucks. He's entitled to know. Well, that's it palsy ... on your way. When we meet again, I'll buy you a cigar."

Still not moving, Anson asked, "How did the police get on to you, Hogan? Why did they ever imagine you killed Barlowe?"

"Because they were smart enough to come out here and fingerprint the bedroom," Hogan said. "They found my prints: maybe they have found yours, but I have a cast-iron alibi and I bet you haven't been sucker enough yourself not to have a cast-iron alibi."

Anson stood staring at Hogan, cold blood crawling up his spine. "They fingerprinted the bedroom?"

He thought of Jud Jones, and his sneering blackmailing smile.

"They sure did," Hogan said. "Stood me on my ear when Jenson told me."

Anson suddenly felt defeated. He thought of that odd moment when Harmas had produced the glass paperweight. He had been vaguely uneasy about why Harmas had suddenly dropped his probing questions and had produced the paperweight. His heart gave a lurch. He had fallen for one of the oldest police tricks in the world. They now had his fingerprints. They would have found by now plenty of his prints in the dirty, sordid bedroom made during those nights when he had slept with Meg. They now would know that he had been Meg's lover; that, plus Merryweather's evidence, plus the fact he had changed his car tyres could cook him … anyway, they were enough facts for Maddox to swing into action against him!

Maddox!

Anson stood for a long moment, his brain racing, his face turning livid.

Harmas had said Maddox had agreed to pay the claim. So what had he done? He had rushed out there to be sure of his share! Maddox would know he would do just that very thing. What a stupid fool he was! He had walked into a trap. Slowly, he looked around the room. He knew

Maddox's methods. He lifted his hands in a gesture of despair.

Puzzled, Hogan and Meg were watching him, shocked by the sudden change that had come over him.

"Look, palsy ..." Hogan began, then stopped as Anson motioned him to silence.

The two of them watched him move around the room. He pulled aside the sideboard and looked behind it. He began a slow, systematic search of the room. The whiteness of his face and his despairing expression made both Hogan and Meg remain motionless and silent. Finally, Anson discovered the microphone. It was concealed behind the radiator; its wire lead going out of the window and into the darkness of the garden.

Anson stared at the microphone, furious with himself for falling for such a trick.

And I was crazy enough to think I could outwit this devil, Maddox, he thought. Between the three of us, we have now talked ourselves into the gas chamber.

"What the hell's going on?" Hogan demanded, unnerved by the way Anson was acting. "What is it?"

Again Anson motioned him to silence and then he beckoned. Moving cautiously, Hogan approached and Anson pointed to the microphone. He put his hand on Hogan's arm motioning him to say nothing.

Hogan stared at the microphone as if it was a deadly snake. Sweat burst out on his battle scarred face. Meg moved forward. When she saw the microphone, she stifled a scream.

Hogan turned on her viciously and slapped her across the face, sending her reeling back.

"You smart, stupid bitch!" he yelled at her. "Look at that! So you thought you could fix it!"

"Stop it," Anson said. He walked heavily over to the fire and bending down he thrust his hands towards the flames. He felt cold and sick. "Well, it didn't come off," he went on, staring into the fire. "At least, it wasn't a bad try. If this stupid woman had only told me the truth ... if she had admitted she had a record, I'd never have gone ahead with this thing. As soon as Maddox knew what she was, he set this trap and we've walked into it. He never intended to pay the claim. This was his trick to get me out here and set us all talking. We're on tape! We have talked ourselves into the gas chamber!"

"Not me!" Hogan snarled, wiping his sweating face. "I have an alibi! They can't touch me! To hell with you two! I'm in the clear!"

Meg turned on him; her face white and terrified.

"Jerry! I did this for you! You were going to have the money! You agreed! You can't walk out on me now. I love you! We've got to face this together!"

Hogan's face was now a frightened, white mask.

"Love? You? Do you imagine I ever wanted anything to do with you, you cheap whore, except what I could get out of you? I was planning to take the money and then I would have ditched you! I have all the women I want without getting snarled up with a dead-beat floosie like you. You and your sucker can go to hell!"

"Keep talking," Anson said in a cold, flat voice. "It's all being recorded. Just keep talking."

Neither Hogan nor Meg bothered to listen to what he said. Meg had run over to Hogan and had caught hold of him. He threw her off.

"Get away from me!" Hogan snarled, and he started for the door.

Anson's hand closed around the butt of Barlowe's gun. He pulled it from his pocket and offered it to Meg.

"Kill him," he said. "He isn't fit to live!"

Hogan whirled round as Meg, gripping the gun, lifted it and pointed it at him. His face went slack with fright as he stared at the gun in Meg's hand.

"No! Don't do it!" he exclaimed, his voice shooting up. "Meg!"

"Your yellow boyfriend," Anson said softly and reaching forward, he took the gun from Meg's shaking hand. The sight of the terror on Hogan's face did much to repay that moment in the garage when Hogan had terrified him.

Hogan backed away, sweat running down his face, his breath coming in heavy gasps. As he moved unsteadily into the lobby, the front door bell rang.

Anson said quietly, "Here they are; Jenson, Harmas and the rest of them."

Hogan came back into the sitting-room. He looked wildly around.

"Let them in," Anson said, smiling at him. He was now very quiet and calm. "Then try to talk yourself out of all this. You won't! Nor will she! You both have said enough to put you in the gas chamber ... go ahead ... let them in!"

As the front door bell rang again, Anson put the barrel of the gun into his mouth, and still smiling at Hogan, pulled the trigger.